T811

550 811823

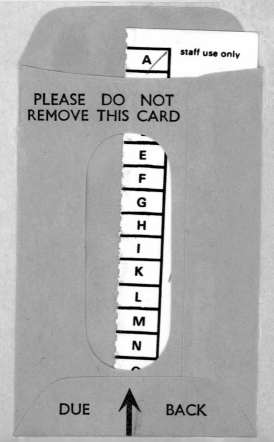

GW00467974

CAMDEN PUBLIC LIBRARY
SWISS COTTAGE LIBRARY,
88 AVENUE ROAD,
LONDON, NW3 3HA

Telephone: 01-278 4444 Ex.3012

(**Recordacall** for book renewals only **01-586 0565**)

This book is due for return on or before the date last stamped on the date card below. If not required by other readers, it may be renewed once by post or telephone. For a subsequent renewal the book must be returned for re-issue.

Fines are charged on overdue books.

(N.B. The cards in the pocket below must not be removed from the book.)

A / staff use only

PLEASE DO NOT
REMOVE THIS CARD

E
F
G
H
I
K
L
M
N

DUE ↑ BACK

A DISTANT
LIKENESS

by the same author

AT THE JERUSALEM

TRESPASSES

Paul Bailey

A DISTANT
LIKENESS

JONATHAN CAPE
THIRTY BEDFORD SQUARE LONDON

First published 1973
© Paul Bailey 1973

Jonathan Cape, 30 Bedford Square, London WCI

ISBN 0 224 00863 3

F
T811823
A

Printed and bound in Great Britain
by W. & J. Mackay Limited, Chatham

For Oliver Reynolds

THE MAN who sniffed out Albert Hawker left his bed before daybreak. Palms pressed together, fingers interlocked, he prayed to the God he no longer believed in for an end to his pain. Then he laughed at himself and his hands returned to his sides.

He sat by the window, waiting for light.

There was no wife in his bed, no Pamela, no warmth. That sheet, tangled now, might have been his shroud: he had dreamed of dying. No mourners followed the cart along the road.

The first one was a slender girl with golden hair.

– Your young eyes will see worse sights than this before the night's over.

The second was a Russian who had put a revolver to his mouth. The bullet had gone through his head and out of the window. It was found in the yard when the snow melted.

– There were these three nuns took a day off from the convent.

The third and fourth were husband and wife. They were old and thin. They lay alongside a gas oven with photograph albums beneath their heads.

The last that night was a woman who looked like a man. She had made her noose out of six regimental ties. Buller stopped telling him funny stories:

7

– Poor Arthur. I knew her well. She was a good soul underneath.

Each slow step brought him nearer to Mrs Emerald and her mulled wine. London contained nothing but the dead. Ghosts stalked past him in the streets. The branches of trees were putrefying arms. He saw the Christmas star above those arms and remembered his mother. Lux fulgebit hodie super nos: perhaps she was at peace now with her bloody angels. She had died in a white bed, with starched nurses creaking about her. The tears he had willed to remain behind his eyes had fallen when she cursed him.

Mrs Emerald wrapped the dolls he had bought for Buller's plump twin daughters in fancy paper. One day, as soon as his wild oats were sown, he would be giving toys to his own little ones, she said.

They were living things, and warm. They played with him and pulled at his clothes and dressed him in red and called him Santa. Their wet kisses soothed him.

There was another ghost, his arse a red forest. Pamela moaned contentedly. Her nails clawed the flesh on the ghost's back.

Now he wondered – as he straightened the tangled sheet so that his hands could be occupied – why he had stared. They had struggled here and he had watched. Their cries had not inflamed him – they were sounds, like others.

He went through his exercises. He liked to keep his body lean and strong.

8   *

Lily had red hair. It was Titian. Her room had a greasy smell: she worked by candlelight. Benny waited on the landing.

— You can't kiss me. If you try once more, young man, you'll get the hot end of my fag in your gob.

He heard Benny stamping his feet outside. It was a cold winter.

— You like your tit, don't you? Didn't your mother give you enough? You're not having my jumper off, so you can just stop trying. I only give the full service when the weather's mild.

He sucked the wool. She took his head in her big hands and lifted it away from her. She told him to put his hard thing where he'd paid for it to go.

This hair was black. He stared. She laughed and the cigarette dropped on to the bed. He returned it to her mouth.

— Who ever heard of a lady dyeing her hole Tishun?

No mystery, he heard; nothing to solve. Some bloke, name of Belsey, had run amok. One of those family massacres. This Belsey had probably had a brainstorm.

He drove through sunlit streets to the scene of the crime. Sometimes the dead whore kept him company; once, passing The Load of Hay, it was the voice of the living ghost that came to him, suggesting malt whisky.

In this part of London you saw all races, all colours. In this street, it was said, only the funeral parlour belonged to an Englishman.

The boys from the school surrounded him, a jeering pack. They shouted:
– Spaghetti! Spaghetti!
– Frank's a wop! Frank's a bloody Eytie!
– He's nearly black and he calls himself White!
Or they sang:
– "Oh, oh, Antonio, he's gone away ... "
They grew into nothings, nobodies. He was the hunter now.

Belsey was smiling.
'His face hasn't changed since we've been here,' said Constable Gregory.
'It soon will. I'll make it change. Take him away.'
Belsey put his arms out for the constables.
One painting was of dots, another of triangles, a third of stripes. A bronze cube rested on a pedestal.

They had lived in this part of London.
– We shall be happy here, Nora.
– Don't you start by putting a curse on the place. We'll be happy if it's the Lord's will, otherwise not. The sooner those cases are unpacked the sooner we'll be settled.
Then Jesus Carrying the Lamb went up, and the picture of the Virgin. A new home was declared open. David smiled at Nora: they were safe again for a time. The little one would make new friends.
– Poverino.
Though English like roast beef, he always used the strange words when he sensed that his son was

unhappy; when he told his son to close his eyes:
– Dormi, poverino.

He ordered the younger constable to water the geraniums. Flowers should be tended.

'Why are they here?'

'To brighten the place, sir.'

'Let them brighten it then.'

He looked at Belsey, who smiled.

'Why are you smiling, Mr Belsey? Tell me. Are you thinking of something funny?'

Belsey laughed.

'That's the first noise you've made since we met this morning. We seem to be progressing. Perhaps, in time, you will speak to me as well. I'm patient. I can wait.'

Belsey unclasped his hands and mimed a pen passing slowly over paper.

'Say it.'

Belsey repeated the mime.

'You wish to write a message?'

Belsey nodded.

'Why not say it instead?'

He took Belsey's moving hand and held it firmly. 'Wipe the smile away and speak.'

Belsey grinned. Gold flashed briefly.

He gave Belsey a notebook and pencil. Belsey wrote: No More Words.

'Put him in a cell. Take away anything he can use on himself. We don't want to find him dead in the morning.'

*

He read that a mother and son had been stabbed to death. A man was helping the police with their inquiries.

The waiter brought him a steak.

He struggled with a piece of gristle and saw her as she had been that evening. Her looks had unnerved him. He had spoken to her hair, her throat, her shoulders.

Although he was hungry he could eat no more.

To float on that calm water ...

Lithe, brown children – the youngest of them naked – swam in the bay. They shouted or sang the strange words. He longed to join them.

Now the sun was red. It bounced on the sea in the far distance. His mother called from the beach that she wouldn't care, no she'd laugh she would, if he was to perish of pneumonia.

He felt no pain when she slapped the backs of his legs. What if a great wave had come and swept him off? He would soon have been meat for the fishes then.

– I'm happy.

Merciful Father, that she should have brought into this world a boy who could declare he was happy in the midst of a shivering fit.

– I am.

He tried to smile but his teeth wouldn't let him. He begged her to bring him to Margate again.

He stopped at a pub and bought a bottle of whisky.

*

Melissa wondered if the Chevalier de Rouget would ever arrive at the castle. What had he said to her that night at Dover? 'I will cross the seas again to claim you, my love.' She saw him now, golden-tanned in his brown doublet,

Before Pamela there had been only tarts, the trash of the streets. Shame always followed: a smell; an itch that had to be scrubbed away. He'd kept a special soap, a great red slab, to use on his love nights. *his black cloak caught by the March wind as he boarded his ship 'L'aurore'. (She could almost hear him saying 'L'aurore' in his lilting Parisian accent.) His faithful comrades had given her, Melissa, a salute of twelve cannon.*

This morning, needing release, he had remembered fat Lily.

The ship had disappeared from the horizon by the dawn's light. ('L'aurore, it means the dawn, my love,' he had whispered before planting the last, hurried kiss on her eager, waiting lips.) Watching it go, a sharp pang bit at her heart, gnawing at her very soul.

A bomb finished Lily – her greasy room, her Titian hair.

'That's it, old lad.' This would be his last glass, his last indulgence. There were enough wrecks littering the world.

– Let me be your ghost.

He drank.

It was a balmy night. The moon was full.

13

He stopped. This place was familiar to him, yet for some reason he had forgotten his way.

He took the road which veered to the left. The moonlight became faint. His hands, groping in front of him, touched the bars of a cage.

He looked inside. A monstrous shape came towards him, sighing. He moved on. He passed other monsters in other cages. Their sighs guided him through the darkness.

He seemed to be in open country: there was space all around him. The wind sounded like great wings flapping.

A lion or leopard or perhaps a wild cat crouched on the grass. He saw its eyes, its whiskers, and screamed. The creature backed away in fear.

He had drunk too much. The bedroom returned. At least he hadn't met a pink elephant.

Piper made a fist and the canary's life came to an end. Hill looked at his dead bird and began to weep.

– Murderer, he whispered.

– What did you call me?

– I called you a murderer.

– That's ripe. Did you hear him, Frank?

– I heard.

– He's done for two women and he stands there and says –

– Be quiet. Calm down. They lose control, not us.

– I'm sorry.

– Keep one thing in mind. That nasty runt is innocent until he's been proved guilty.

14

This was no one's smooth skin, these were nobody's breasts.

They followed Sidney Pickard into the parlour. He asked them to be thoughtful and not raise their voices. His wife was taking her afternoon rest upstairs.

— I see we have a new young man here today.

— This is Frank, Mr Pickard, said Benny.

— Pleased to meet you, Frank. You look a strong fellow. Oh my, indeed you do. Help yourself to tuck.

He took a cream bun from the cake stand on the table. Mr Pickard poured him a glass of lemonade.

— Draw the curtains, Peter. Games must commence sharp on four o'clock.

Mr Pickard rolled up his shirt-sleeves and removed his wedding ring.

— Don't drink so much, Ronald. It will spoil our fun if you have to be excused.

Mr Pickard opened the sideboard and brought out a china pig. He shook it and said:

— Who's going to be first today?

Peter Lawson went to the special chair. He sat back in it and allowed Mr Pickard to undo his trouser buttons. Benny laughed.

— Behave yourself. Show a little respect.

— Yes, Mr Pickard.

— As for you, Peter, I'm ashamed of you. Look how dirty he is. Make sure you wash him properly before you come again. Take your threepence out of Porky, even though you don't deserve it. Who's next?

— You go, Frank.

— Now just sit back and be comfortable. Hands off,

15

Frank — you mustn't keep him all to yourself. Oh my, he's a chap to be reckoned with. Yes, yes ... I'm going to call him Heathcliff.

  — Who's he?

  — A wild, wild lad. A young terror. Ronald's turn.

  — Enjoy your wank, Frank?

  — I will not tolerate filthy language, Peter. Your mind seems to be as much in need of a scour as your body. Show a little decency.

They did impersonations of Mr Pickard whenever Tarzan made lovey-dovey with Jane in the tree-tops.

The cart tipped him into blackness and he awoke. Earth still fell on him. He sat up. He touched the lamp, then the table it stood on. He turned on the light and flicked open Pamela's historical romance: lovely Melissa was in her castle, waiting for the Chewhatnot de Doodah to return. He pressed the whisky bottle against his cheek. The word 'God' stuck in his throat.

No — no prayers; no blessings from Him. They could go where the altars, the incense, the rosaries, the old dead language had gone. Where his mother, whom he'd tried to protect from that fool who was English like roast beef — yes, they could go wherever she was. He was done with such nonsense.

Flames licked his lean, strong body as he fell asleep.

ENOUGH WRECKS littered the world. He swallowed two of Pamela's aspirins. He went slowly through his exercises.

The tight bastard was himself again. He decided to wear his Albert Hawker tie.

On just such a bright day they had lowered his mother into the ground. The resurrection and the life were items on the priest's shopping-list, ticked off as they were delivered.

'Come on, old lad. Work to do.'

He whistled as he drove.

'Did he say thank you for his breakfast?'

'No, sir.'

'Did he eat it?'

'Licked the plate clean, sir.'

'I'm sure he did. You can tell by his gut that he's fond of his grub.'

Belsey patted his stomach.

'You'll harm your digestion.'

Belsey stood up. He farted loudly and sat down.

'Let's hear from the other end.'

Belsey shook his head.

He heard the magistrate charge James Harold Belsey with the murders of Marian Jane Belsey and Alan Belsey. The accused was to be remanded in custody for psychiatric and medical tests.

The words would spill out, the smile would vanish.
  − It's as if you loved them.

− So my big little son is joining the police, is he?
  − It's a job.
  − And you'll be great at it. In your element. Dragging them in and putting them down.
  − Would you rather I ended up like him?
  She came close to him and smiled. She stared at him for an age.
  − Yes. I would much rather you did.

The children walked over the crossing and into the park.
  The specialist said:
  − I'm afraid, Mr White − Inspector − I'm afraid I must ask you to do something of a private nature.
  − What is it, Dr Cottie?
  The specialist lowered his voice, even though no one else was present:
  − I must ask you to − to manipulate him. Your person, that is ... Into this test-tube. In the other room, of course.
  He went into the other room. There was a large

photograph of Lyme Regis at the turn of the century on one of the brown walls.

He put the test-tube into his left hand and began. He closed his eyes and imagined Pamela naked.

He looked down. He had made no progress.

He watched the bustled beauties of Lyme Regis as they halted on the front, on a glorious August morning, and stripped for him. He helped them out of their corsets: flesh flopped into his hands. He rolled on the beach with them, knocking sandcastles over.

Wild, wild Heathcliff was in a stubborn mood today.

– I can't.

– What I'd advise, in that case, is that you take the tube home with you. Fill it up for me, if you can, and let me have it back tomorrow. Put the cap on it and bring it straight round. Give it to my receptionist. Then it will be plain sailing.

Several car horns were being sounded.

'Poor Jim. Poor Jim.'

There were no words, Daniels said, no words at all.

A small fist beat the air three times.

After a silence Daniels said he'd like to make it clear that it went without saying how shocked, how horrified he was. You only read about such things.

Jim had been – my, my, there he was, using the past tense already – well, he had been an ideal partner. If he had a fault as a person – and which person is faultless? – it was his tendency to become impatient with people. He did not suffer fools gladly.

'Whereas I do. I have to. I'm not saying our

20

clients and staff are fools, but we get a fair proportion of them, if you follow me. I've cultivated the velvet touch.'

A small hand stroked the air some inches above the large table.

Jim would flare up at times – especially when another firm had pipped them to the post, which hadn't happened often he was glad to report; yes indeed, Jim would really go on the rampage, on the warpath, on those blessedly few occasions – but he had never seen him in a depressed state. Depressions, moods, soul-searchings –

Small fingers pulled at a quiff.

– those were luxuries Jim had denied himself.

Leastways, that was the case as far as he knew. There was always a limit to your knowledge of your fellow human beings, wasn't there? Even a shrewd judge of human nature like himself – to hell with false modesty, he made his living out of his ability to sum people up, and though he said it himself he had very rarely been wrong, very rarely – even he had to admit the distressing truth: you could see just so far into a man's character and no farther. Up against a barrier you came: smack!

The small fist hit a small palm.

Now he thought about it, there had been only two types of people in Jim's view – the useful and the useless. Mind you, if he was honest, he would have to concede that he was of the same opinion. He was a diplomat, though; Jim wasn't. He knew the value of charm.

The value of leisure he knew about, too. A good book, music. You had to let your mind escape sometimes. He himself collected water-colours, soothing scenes of the English countryside.

Oh, those stripes and triangles and dots of Jim's, they were investments, bought on the best advice. They were security. The man who could see beauty in them was an intellectual or a crank or both. His own water-colours were worth a pretty penny, too – there wasn't a dud among them – but they meant something to him as well. You couldn't imagine Jim's pictures quietening your nerves at the end of an exhausting day. Food and drink – Jim's interests, passions rather, outside his work – weren't enough in the long run.

Poor Jim wouldn't be drinking his beloved brandy wherever they were sending him, would he?

To be absolutely serious, in deadly earnest, and although he was only hazarding a guess, which was all you could possibly do in the circumstances – well, perhaps the root of the problem was in the family. Perhaps it lay in the fact that they weren't – what was the expression? – closely knit. Jim never talked of his wife and children – and if anyone deserved to go, God forgive him for saying such a thing at such a terrible time, it was that awful freak of a daughter, Lucy – no, he never brought out snaps from his wallet, like most fathers; never told you stories about his home.

'One thing about my race – and I sometimes think it's almost the only thing about it; we're a vulgar lot on the whole, just you go to one of our weddings if you need proof – we know how to stick together.'

He waited for the small mouth to open again.

'Jim and me came up from the bottom. I myself

22

came up from the rock bottom. Jim despised – despises – his origins, whereas I don't. I never knew he had a mother until she passed on. There's a father around, but I doubt if there's any love between them. Now me – I've got a mother. She's all I have got, if you don't count several thousand sponging relations. I don't have a wife, don't want one; the field's nice enough for playing in, if you follow me. As I say, I've got a mother. I consider her. I bought her a lovely little house on the coast, beautiful garden, every convenience. I pay all her bills for her – the silly old dear, a shocking state she gets into whenever one comes in. She doesn't like to think of me losing any of my money. All in all, I suppose, I must spend about two thousand a year on her – and only seventy-five of that I can claim against my tax. But do I begrudge it? It goes without saying I don't. I regard it as two thousand pounds well spent.'

No, Jim had nothing to worry about – well, not financially.

A man's mind, though, a man's mind; that was something else, that was something else.

This part of London was like a waste land now. Towers would rise here soon, divided by squares for the winter winds to lurch across.

– Am I still in the world?

She saw him.

– Yes.

He found the house. He knocked at the door. He

23

waited. He pushed the letter-box open and saw a hallstand: the smell of fish replaced the smell of roses.

He knocked a second time, and a third.

'It's that bloody Jehovah's Witness again. I told you last time what I'd do to you if you came back here to pester me. I'll show you a lake of bloody fire if I come out there, I can tell you. Piss off.'

'Is that you, Mr Belsey?'

'Never you mind who I am. You take your Almighty elsewhere.'

'Mr Charles Oswald Belsey?'

The old man had crept up to the door. He could hear him breathing.

'Are you the fishmonger?' He gave no answer. 'The boy brought me the kippers hours ago. I gave him the money for them, I can prove it, I made him sign a slip of paper.'

'I'm a policeman, Mr Belsey. A detective inspector.'

'I haven't been after that black man. No, I haven't been after him since you warned me at the station. I've seen nobody. I haven't left these four walls of mine for months. I tell you no lie. You leave me in peace. You just let me alone. I swear to you I've been law-abiding ever since.'

'I wish to speak to you.'

'What you doing now – clog dancing?'

'I should like to exchange a few words with you, Mr Belsey. Face to face.'

'I'm going to die where I've lived and no place else. It won't be so long. They can knock the house down once I've gone out of it feet first.'

'It's about your son.'

'His Lordship?'

'James Harold Belsey.'

'He's not going to have me put away, however hard he tries. I don't care where it is, or if they spread caviare on your toast, or even if they bring on the dancing girls of an evening.'

'Your son couldn't put you anywhere. He's lost whatever authority he had.'

'What do you mean?'

'He's in our hands.'

'His Lordship is? Well, well, well. I'm not surprised. No, it's no surprise to me at all. I've maintained all my born days that you can't make a pile of money without being a crook of one kind or another. What is he? Swindler? Forger?'

'Neither.'

'Embezzlement, is it?'

'No.'

'Then what's His Lordship done?'

'If you let me come inside, I'll tell you.'

He listened as the door was unlatched and unbolted.

'Before I open, can I trust you?'

'Yes.'

He faced Belsey's father.

'My name's White. And this is Detective-Constable Nash.'

'I thought there was only one of you.'

The stink of fish grew stronger as they walked down the passage.

He heard himself say, under his breath, 'You trained me, Mother.' The tight bastard was of her making.

'An odd bugger.'

'Yes, sir.'

'Like a hermit.'

'Yes, sir. That's the word.'

Those people strolling in the afternoon sun, those children playing on the dusty common – he was their protector. He moved among them, sniffing out the ones who lost control.

He would clear Pamela's junk from the house: her creams and scents, her chocolates, whatever else. Melissa could wait for her lover where the flies buzzed.

When he had Belsey whining he would look for a flat.

Both the psychiatrist and the lawyer had left the prison with No More Words written on their pads.

'I met your father today.'

Belsey unclasped his hands. He slit his throat from ear to ear with a thumb. He smiled.

'I got the impression he loved you, too. I also made the acquaintance of your partner.'

Belsey repeated the mime.

'He sang your praises. I sat in his office and marvelled. You could say I was struck dumb. The next time you show me your backside, I'll protect my eyes from the glare. I have yet to meet your daughter.'

Belsey made no reply.

'I shall bring her to see you. Lucy will set your tongue working.'

Belsey's knife plunged into the mattress.

This wasn't him. Someone else was inside his skin – someone weak and moony, someone less than a man.

'That's enough, old lad.'

Pamela wasn't the be-all and end-all; there were more fish in the sea. The ghost was welcome to her.

She banged a tambourine near the red forest and sang:

– Come and join us!

He asked for another steak.

She came across the dance floor. She glowed before him.

'I've come to tuck you in for the night. To wish you sweet dreams.'

'He enjoyed his evening meal, sir.'

Belsey licked his lips.

'No food for him tomorrow. His stomach could do with a rest.'

Each part of London seemed to have its own daft old woman. Lottie reigned here. She wore her fur coat in all weathers and seldom carried less than ten bags. These were now on the ground: she was dancing a jig over them. She was celebrating the end of the world, her voice soaring high above the noise of the street.

When her vision had passed, she would cough for a while. Then she would pick up her bags and curse all dirty, rotten men and their filthy, stinking ways.

It wouldn't be long before she was seized by the wondrous spirit again.

He looked in every room. She might have returned. She could be hiding somewhere, waiting to surprise him, playing one of her games. He opened the door of the airing-cupboard.

The house was empty.

And here was the handsome detective – who also wrote books, tasted wines, collected antiques, drove a sports car and rode to hounds; who played chess when a case was proving difficult ('I must get to the airport before something terrible happens!' – forgetting to pawn her bishop; leaving the marchioness with the tits you could put your suitcase on staring after him) – yes, here he was, at the close, receiving the superintendent's growled congratulations: 'I don't know how you do it, Miles. Don't let it go to your head, though. Just remember, it's back to the boring grind in the morning.'

Sipping champagne between kisses, the marchioness and Miles finished their game in bed. Cherubs smiled down on them.

He laughed.

He sat, one of the chosen, in the cold green hall.

They heard the stout inspector say there would be no glory. In the main, and for most of their lives, they would be wading through shit. To cope, to stay sane, meant being disciplined, having patience, exercising control.

— Let me be your ghost.

No glory, no cherubs; no Pamela, no warmth.

He concentrated on the tennis match.

Melissa shed many bitter tears. There was no one to whom she could turn in her hour of need. She fled from the hated castle, the sound of her brutal husband's carousing ringing in her ears. Breathless, she stopped outside the convent gates. Her eyes told her that she was standing before the blessed sanctuary. Her heart told her that there was someone she could turn to after all — the comforter of her childhood, Mother Francesca

Buller's nuns! Their tongues weren't content with holy wafers; not for them the words like stones:

— Dominus vobiscum.

— Et cum spiritu tuo.

No, they were a riotous lot, their habits up over their heads, doing their morning press-ups on the cucumber patch. Or paying sneaky visits, at dead of night, to that tool-shed at the bottom of the monastery garden ...

They scampered in and out of the houses, those wicked girls, and the Christmas star cast a dim light over the earth.

No one was here to echo his sighs.

He would go back to the trash for a while – shag, shag, until his blood was cool once more.

The day wouldn't dawn when he'd be fodder for some trick-cyclist.

'Go to sleep, old lad.'

– You don't live in the real world, Frank. Alec does.

A happy dream. Better still, a night's oblivion.

– Sit up, Mr White. Your son has come to see you.

His father stayed under the sheet.

– Mr White!

– Mi chiamo Esposito.

And the fool who was English like roast beef, the slim stealer of hearts, leapt from the bed. He took the nurse in his fat arms:

– Voglio chiavarti.

– He's talking his gibberish again.

Angels, grant Nora a glimpse of her David now. Send her down for a moment to inspect the ruin.

The nurse freed herself and left the room. He waited for his father to speak.

– Where's your pride gone? That was all you ever had.

Rough hands were always there to push him down. Rocks – boulders, even – could not stop the cart. Its progress was steady. It would reach its destination.

His mother was by the table, shelling peas.

– Don't stare so, Frank. Occupy yourself.

The awful thought had made his arms and legs heavy.

Mr Baldwin would die, and Greta Garbo, and Charlie Chaplin.

– Oh, Frank, stir yourself.

Tarzan's strong body would be dust one day.

Only wrecks drank whisky in the middle of the night.

– Don't you pity any of them?

– Pity never brought anyone back to life. You lose control and you pay the penalty. I'm a before man, not an after.

– Well put, said the ghost.

Imagine: Frank White on his knees and some sod of the cloth talking of mercy. Or picture him begging her to return, promising a fresh start in that real world where the ghost lives.

Listen to him as he joins their ranks, telling the trick-cyclist it was his broken home, it was his childhood, it was the skeleton in the cupboard up in Annie's room behind the clock, it was too much of this and not enough of that: it wasn't his fault; other people were to blame. Listen – pigs are flying overhead.

– Do you ever read detective stories?

– When I want a laugh.

No laughing matter then: not with the rain outside, and Leafy, and the smell of disinfectant coming up from the boards. The burning sands of the

Sahara, tropical islands, the filthy stews of Hong Kong –

– If I pick up a book nowadays, it's got to be a true one. The war, or someone's life story. I was done with the other nonsense years ago.

They had struggled here. He had watched.

No More Words.

'They're going to pour out. I'll see to it. Old lad, there's going to be a flood.'

Frank

Please read this through to the end. Dont tear it up just because its from me. I havent written a letter for years. Well this time I had to write. After all those terrible things that were said I thought pen and paper would calm me down and make me more reasonable.

No hard feelings please Frank. I have a nerve writing that but it pays in the long run not to be bitter. I must have loved you once all though I said the opposite. We all change. Alec says you are dead if you stay the same through out your life.

He had no hand in this please beleive me. You can tell by the way its written. He makes me feel so ignorant. I shall make up for lost time now and start to become an educated woman. Dont laugh. While theres life theres hope and who knows one day I shall be able to hold my own when Alec is talking with clever people.

No more damsels in distress for me says Alec and no knights in shining armor. They are banned from the flat. It is just like being at school again. Imagine it. I am reading Treasure island at the moment. If I must have fantasey Alec says let it be a good one. Yo ho ho and a bottle of rum.

Frank I am trying to get to the point. You may find it painful. You are only human in spite of the way you always have of being cold when it comes to feelings and such. Anyway here goes.

34

*There are 2 things. First of all Frank I want you to
divorce me. God knows you have grounds after what
you saw that day and what we said to you. I honestly
dont care how much muck flies round the court room.
They can call me the biggest tart in the business if
they care to. I do love Alec so much and I want to be
his wife.*

*I am quite prepared to live in sin with him as they say.
But I would rather not because of the second thing. I
am going to have a baby Frank.*

They rolled on the beach that August morning.
Sandcastles crumbled.

*Well better late than never. It sounds like something
out of one of those daft books I use to read but I feel
like a woman at last. Yes I do. Call me old fashoned
but I want the child to have a proper mother even if it
means going to the alter so to speak after he or she is
born.*

*Touch wood and fingers crossed there will be no hitch.
Pray for my sake that nothing goes wrong Frank.
Please. I shall have to go very careful in the months
ahead. I am no chicken to put it mildly. 42 is late in
the day to have your first one. Like mother like
daughter. Well I got there in the end and now you
know. I hope you will be agreeable. If not I can try
mental cruelty. No good can come from us staying
man and wife Frank.*

*I feel better for writing this. Try not to think badly of
me.*

Pamela

London would be like a great oven again.

He did some of his exercises, then took a shower.
He shaved carefully. He dressed. He had his pride.

*

He swam away from her. He looked back once and saw an insect. Soon she would be out of sight.

He was alone in the sea. When he went under, there were no boys yellowing the water and no tiled floors to break his dives. Here, at last, he had space.

It was then that he felt the presence of God. He was someone mightier than the man she had dealings with: this vast ocean was His, and that sky.

It seemed to him in those few happy – but, of course, loony – moments that he was both big and small. He was big with the splendour of the scene and he moved about like a great fish to celebrate it. While his body expanded, the Frank White Mr Leaves said was stupid and lazy shrivelled – and in no time at all was gone.

Cold brought him back, and the thought of dying from pneumonia. He would have to preserve those moments, store them. He would think of them when he was mumbling the stones or taking his threepence out of Porky, or when the boys at school stopped being his mates and turned themselves into a jeering pack. He would try to recall them the next time Macbeth spouted on and on in his castle.

He would need them most when David looked at Nora in that special way.

– I'm happy, he said as she slapped his legs.

She made him drink tea at Margate station. It scalded his tongue. But sea and sky returned, blotting out the woman behind the urn and the cake his mother wouldn't allow him to eat because of his disobedience. The pain didn't matter.

The train wheels said: Don't let them go, Don't let them go ...

36   *

In the interview room he loosened his Albert Hawker tie.

'Bring him up.'

Seymour was the whore expert. Sometime during the day he would seek his advice.

Belsey was brought in.

'How was breakfast?'

Belsey patted his stomach.

'Has he been fed?'

'No, sir.'

— It's as if you loved them.

'I love you, Sonny Jim.'

Belsey blew him a kiss.

'I was taught as a child to love my fellow men.' He spoke loudly, looking at the warder.

Belsey had sat down.

'Get up. Up, up.'

Belsey rose slowly.

Before he could ask the questions he'd prepared, he heard that Belsey's daughter had been traced.

She was drunk when she said:

— I keep thinking of what you've seen. And then you look at me with the same pair of eyes.

— That's gin speaking.

— Bloody corpses, year in, year out.

— Some of them aren't at all bloody.

— You've a lovely sense of humour, too. You'll make me die laughing.

— Go to bed, Pamela, and sleep it off.

— Whatever it is, it will still be there in the morning. I can't sleep this off.

It's come early in her life, he thought. Childless women suffer from the change sooner. He would stay calm during her scenes, hear her out, be patient with her when she stormed and raved. He would bring home little presents.

Her snores kept him awake that night.

Irish and Polish trash were waiting outside a betting shop.

'Lazy bastards.'

Dear old Daddy, that astute man of business, would have been among their number, given half the chance. There were no such places in his heyday. When he fancied a flutter he had to contact one of his associates: Mr Johnson, Mr Foster, Mr Smith —

— Esposito is as common as Smith.

What a roll-call!

'Welcome to the shithouse, sir,' said Nash. 'In more ways than one. I'll be surprised if the drug boys haven't been here.'

The stairs creaked under their feet.

'I prefer the fishy smell at Old Father Time's place.'

They went into a room on the second floor.

'That's her.'

He faced a slender girl with golden hair.

Buller patted him on the shoulder and told him there would be worse sights before the night was over.

She was staring at him.

'Are you Lucy Belsey?'

'I'm just Lucy.'

'And what does that mean?'

'I don't care to have a family name.'

'You can't get by without one.'

'I use it as little as possible.'

'Do you know why we're here?'

'I don't know why you're anywhere.'

'Have you seen the papers?'

'Why concern myself with lies?'

'What I have to tell you is horribly true.'

She continued to stare at him.

'Your father has murdered your mother and your brother.'

She made no response.

'Very brutally. With a knife.'

She spoke eventually. 'So?'

Stripes, dots and triangles decorated the slaughterhouse.

Her eyes were still on him.

'Look what the cat's dragged in,' said Nash. He turned. A young man stood in the doorway.

'Who are you?'

'Ben Gunn, I should think.'

'Who's Ben Gunn, Nash?'

'You know, sir. That mad git with all the hair. In Treasure Island.'

'Never read it.'

He asked Lucy Belsey if the dumb hairy streak with the earring was her lover.

'We fuck.'

'You do?'

'Yes. We do. So?'

'So you should try a mouth wash.'

'Should I?'

'You seem to be in need of one. So what about your father?'

She shrugged. 'So what about him?'

'Christ Almighty, hasn't it sunk in yet? What he's done?'

'People in his world – your world – do things like that. It happens all the time. You should know.'

– Every man loves his neighbour, lives and lets live ...

'Your mother. Your brother. Your own flesh and blood.'

He waited for a reply.

'You don't feel any grief? None? You've no pity?'

'Everyone's made of flesh and blood. I pity the victims of their society, not them. My mother and brother, as you call them – to me they're other people – had a choice. They chose your way.'

'And which way is that?'

'A way which needs men like you. I'm not happy they're dead, but it happens.'

'You're an iceberg. You're a marble slab.'

'You'll never understand.'

'I need a change of scenery.' He looked at the young man. 'Do you share her opinions?'

The young man nodded.

'Come on, Nash.'

'Go in peace,' said Lucy Belsey.

He surprised himself by asking Nash to call him Frank.

40

'You'll be my equal soon enough, Eric.'

He could see Nash having a jar with his friends, telling them how the tight bastard had suddenly revealed a chink in his armour. Wonders would never cease.

'Let's have a quick one at this pub.'

'Seymour?'

'Speaking.'

'White.'

'Which one?'

'Frank White. Inspector.'

'Ah, yes.'

'Can you give me some advice?'

'If it's vice advice I can.'

'Yes. Can you recommend a whore?'

'Wife off somewhere?'

'Yes. Long holiday. This heat's got me horny as a bull. I've been told you know the wheat from the chaff.'

'What sort do you want?'

'The wheat, naturally.'

'No, what type? Any particular preference?'

'Not fussy. Dark or fair's no matter. Just so long as I can stuff her with my eyes open.'

'I'll just consult my little book. Wait a tick.'

Seymour gave him the address and telephone number of a frisky kitten.

Tonight, perhaps, the cart wouldn't make the journey. His blood cool, he would sleep like any other satisfied man. It was something to hope for.

Even Hill had wept for a canary.

It was on just such a bright day that his tears had fallen when she cursed him.

Regrets were nonsense: at his age he should be done with them.

'And I shall be.'

He whistled as he told her that he had not been a bad son. Thanks to him, the fool wasn't where he deserved to be – in some doss-house, discussing high finance with his former associates.

– Dormi, poverino.

Those other upright citizens. Imagine!

'A lovely girl. A daughter to be proud of.'

Belsey smiled.

'Aren't you going to show me what you wanted to do to her?'

Gold flashed.

'Write it then.'

Belsey wrote his usual message.

He was shivering in the great oven. He was standing on the mean strip of grass outside the prison, his body shaking with cold.

The sound of his laugh could not get past his teeth.

He had tried to make the ghost understand. He was a before man, not an after – without control, society would founder.

– You have the nose for it, boy, said Buller.

One of the chosen, he sat in the cold green hall. The rain falling into the yard looked thick and black. The inspector walked up and down and told them about the shit he had waded through:

– Your faces have gone the colour of the walls. You'll need stronger stomachs, that's for sure.

Buller helped him out of the red curtain in which he had been Santa.

– You'll succeed, boy. I've yet to be wrong.

Those same streets contained the living. He walked among them. Lazy, stupid Frank White had an aim in life, a mission almost: he was a hunter now.

– It's as if you loved them.

Imagine: love!

Alec Turner had sniffed him out.

– Let me be your ghost.

The questions, the flattery, the promises – the whole bloody works.

– He doesn't take me for granted, Frank.

People change.

What future awaited him? It was better not to think about it; it was better simply to live. What had been, what was to come: no one in his senses had time for such matters.

43

He took off his jacket and rolled up his shirt-sleeves.

He was wondering what the triangles meant when the photographer said:

— It's worse than a furnace in here.

The Belsey dining-room had a glass roof.

— It's time the weather broke. A good downpour would clear the air a bit.

The remains of breakfast were on the steel table.

— I hope there won't be any thunder and lightning though.

A wasp flew into the marmalade pot.

— It's ridiculous. If there's one thing guaranteed to scare the living daylights out of me, it's a thunderstorm. If I'm at home when one starts, I have to hide in the cupboard under the stairs where the cat sleeps.

He looked at the photographer.

— Does your wife laugh when you hide?

— Enough to scare a hyena.

She wouldn't be laughing today.

Whistling, he drove through the waste land.

Was this Pamela screaming?

— I want friends, I want conversation. Before it's too late.

— I'm not stopping you. The whole world's out there waiting for you to make friends with it. Pull yourself together.

How fat she's become, he thought. How ugly.

She came across the dance floor, glowing. He spoke to her hair, her throat, her shoulders.

He was fascinated. He watched. Their cries weren't inflaming him – they were sounds, like others.

The red forest swayed on the snowy plain.

The noise the tambourine was making told him where he was.

'I'm not the Jehovah's Witness.'

'Who are you then?'

'My name's White. I spoke to you yesterday.'

'It's today now.'

'I want to speak to you again.'

'His Lordship on the run, is he?'

'No. He's still in a safe place.'

'What do you want then?'

'I just told you.'

After a while the door was unlatched and unbolted. He went into the house.

'Not staying long, are you?'

'That isn't a nice welcome.'

'Why in hell should I welcome you?'

Dust rose as he sat down.

'Is there a reason why those pictures are turned to the wall?'

'That's my business.'

'You've got a fish-bone stuck to your chin.'

'And there's clinkers stuck to my arsehole, too. What do you want?'

'To speak to you.'

'I haven't time to waste, even if you have.'

'What keeps you occupied? Housework?'

'That's the butler's job.'

'I'd tell him to sling his hook. He's less than use-less.'

'I don't want to see His Lordship, if that's what you're here about.'

'You were off your rocker not so long ago, weren't you?'

'Was I? Who says?'

'You behaved like an idiot.'

'Did I? I had some cause to.'

'Pestering those blacks.'

'It was only one.'

'I'm afraid it wasn't. Couldn't you tell them all apart?'

'I haven't been out of these four walls of mine for months.'

'I know. Just as well. Imagine – one of them might have turned really nasty. You could have been somebody's dinner.'

'Like an ape, he was.'

'Describe him.'

'Big. Black. He was.'

'I see him perfectly ... They told me at the station here that six different coloured men complained about you. One was Nigerian, another West Indian. And one of them was a pansy, on the game, known locally as Samantha.'

'I'll die here.'

'He thought you were a customer until you called him a murdering bastard.'

'No other place.'

'That's what they told me, anyway.'

'I've been law-abiding since. I made a vow I wouldn't go out of here.'

'Not even for food?'

'No. The milkman brings me milk and tea. And the fishmonger's boy comes round of a Tuesday with my kippers.'

'And meat?'

'Haven't touched it since I came back.'

'From where?'

'Flanders.'

'Ah.'

'Vegetables is too much trouble. I stick a kipper under the flames and it's done in a couple of shakes.'

'Of course.'

'I'm not saying I don't fancy other fish. Odd times I might feel like some hake or some mackerel. Or sprats, when they're about. Them I was always partial to. But I can't be bothered these days. And anyhow, they'd never taste the same.'

'The same? As what?'

'The same as when she cooked them.'

'Your wife?'

'Yes. My wife. We used to wash them down with a glass of sweet stout.'

'What do you wash your kippers down with?'

'Old Nick's piss. Tea, if it's made. Otherwise nothing. Learnt enough, have you?'

'No.'

He walked across to the window.

'I admire your garden, I must say. It's beautiful.'

'It was.'

'It still is.'

'It used to be something special. The weeds can take over now.'

'You don't tend it?'

'I'm not dead-heading a single flower this year. Oh, there's no bloody point. The moment I've let out my last gasp those money-grubbing swine will be in here with their cement bags and bulldozers. I didn't cope with a wilderness for their benefit.'

'I want to walk in it.'

'You've outstayed your welcome.'

'I didn't get one, if you remember.'

He followed the old man into the passage and waited while he unlatched and unbolted the back door.

The stink of fish was replaced by the smell of honeysuckle.

'Is that a tool-shed?'

'You must have been brought up in a palace if you don't know what that is. In there's where I blow my winds and crack my cheeks. That's the powder room.'

'The toilet.'

'The boudoir, she always said.'

A bird started to sing.

'There he is. What's the time?'

'Six.'

'Punctual as ever. You could set your clock by him.'

'What kind is it?'

'You mean to say you don't know?'

'Yes. That is what I mean to say.'

'He's a thrush.'

'Thank you.'

'I get lots of birds here. Sparrows, naturally.

48

Starlings come, and blackbirds, and robins in the winter. You'll never see a pigeon here, though.'

'Why?'

'Because the pigeons know they're not wanted, that's for why. I scared them off years back. I could never bear the perishing things. Shit and shag's their motto. Yes, shitting and shagging is all they do all their lives. The others you can listen to.'

'I've met your granddaughter.'

'What am I supposed to do? Give you a medal?'

'Are you fond of her?'

'She was a pretty child. I only saw her a few times, but I recall she was pretty.'

'She didn't seem to care. About what's happened.'

'No?'

'Was she upset when your wife died?'

'If she was, I was kept in the dark.'

'She lives with a wild-looking streak. Ben Gunn, one of the lads called him.'

'I must go and do my meal.'

'I might come and see you again.'

'Your life's your own.'

He heard that Lucy Belsey had identified the bodies. There had been no tears. She had twitched slightly when the sheets were lifted, but that was all.

The steak would put lead in his pencil.

— You're so handsome, Frank.

She asked him about the women in his life: there must have been dozens.

49

– There were a few.

Every one a pillar of virtue. Nice girls, but not as nice as Pamela Clayton. He doubted if he'd loved any of them.

No shame, to hear him then; no great red slab to remove its traces.

In this part of London they kept the churches locked. Imagine some poor sinner wanting to do penance, to amend his life, this very minute: some boozy wreck, like those on the bench there, beating against that bolted door, getting no answer.

He found the frisky kitten's residence – the ground-floor flat in a newly painted house. A voice told him to step inside.

'Are you the frisky kitten?'

She was wearing a leopard-skin dress. It made a crackling sound when she moved.

'That's me.'

He'd dropped his trousers in worse places.

The frisky kitten crackled towards the light. He saw that she was really a battered moggy in middle age.

'Straight or discipline?'

'Straight.'

'That'll give my arm a rest. Want me to dress up?'

He heard himself ask, 'As a nun?'

The frisky kitten's laugh was surprisingly deep. She became serious: 'I couldn't do that, love. My heart wouldn't be in it. I respect religion, you see, in spite of my work. You can have a schoolmarm, or a nurse, a girl guide or a ballet dancer. Any of those suit you?'

'No.'

'None of my mates ever does nuns. But I can make inquiries for you, if you like.'

'I wouldn't bother. It was only an idea.'

'I wouldn't earn a penny if people didn't have those. Straight, then, is it?'

'Yes.'

'I don't mind doing oral.'

'No. The straight would suit me best.'

She was crouching on the bed, without her spots. He undressed. He piled his clothes neatly on a chair.

No cherubs beamed down on them.

He would shoot his load quickly.

'Did you get me off the tobacconist's board?'

'You were recommended to me.'

'Who by?'

A man with an odd sense of humour.

He said the name and her pleasant manner vanished instantly.

'You the law?'

'Yes.'

'You expect this free, I suppose?'

'I'll pay you what you're worth.'

'Get on with it.'

'I'm only human.'

He clutched what there was of her breasts.

The kitten frisked as he entered. He pushed twice. It was over. He continued pushing.

He imitated a cry of pleasure.

He left the bed. He dressed. He took several small coins out of his pocket and put them on the counterpane.

'Buy yourself a saucer of cream.'

*

51

– Whatever happens, Buller said, we'll always need your kind.

Enough wrecks littered the world. He would not lose control, like Piper.

He snapped back at the ghost:

– My kind will always be necessary, whatever happens.

He scrubbed his lean, strong body.

'Has he uttered?'

'No, sir.'

'Good evening, Your Lordship.'

Belsey nodded and smiled.

'Guts growled yet?'

Belsey patted his stomach.

'I'm patient. I can wait. You'll be fit to plead.'

– Mi chiamo Esposito.

'You weren't deserted.'

– He's talking his gibberish again.

'That's his way.'

Sandra. Doreen. Jennifer. Angela. Jane.

He was of use. He drank.

Touch wood and fingers crossed there will be no hitch.
Pray for my sake that nothing goes wrong Frank.
Please. I shall have to go very careful

52

She was eating what she called her 'television snack'. He sat down next to her.

– I'm caught up in the film.

They watched together.

Merle Oberon – in a terrible state – called out for Heathcliff.

He tried to suppress his laughter.

– Take your threepence out of Porky.

– Why are you laughing, Frank?

– Nothing ... Nothing.

Mrs Pickard said she would wait for her husband. He was a good man. He was a firm believer in education.

I am the man who sniffed out Albert Hawker. Readers of the (insert name of newspaper) will remember who he is.

He returned the manuscript to the desk.

– We'll sell it to one of the barmaids' bibles.

Behind him were trees, houses, grass, birds ascending. He could not turn his head to see them.

The cart moved slowly on.

It was already day when he awoke.

'Why me?'

He looked down at the street. No rocks, no boulders. People were going to work.

THE REAL WORLD.

He swallowed the last of Pamela's aspirins before going through his exercises.

A legless boy was begging in the subway.

– This place is a hell on earth, Frank. Please let's go back to Rome.

While she packed, he went down to look at the sea. Lithe, brown children, some of them naked, swam in the bay. They shouted and sang the strange words. He longed to join them.

He threw them coins. The foundlings leaped and dived.

No one would know what was happening inside the tight bastard. Imagine him, another Piper, caving in.

'They lose control, not us.'

Let her try mental cruelty. Let her tell the court how wicked he'd been, how inconsiderate.

'She'll have to rack her brains. My God, she will.'

Sandcastles crumbled.

He would not be less than a man. He'd been that only once in his life.

– Am I still in the world?

She saw him.

– Yes.

– Mother.

And then the curses, the fist raised, the spit, the thin body shaking.

And his tears.

'Catch me crying for her.'

He was in good shape, no doubt about it. He was as lean and fit as any athlete.

– I want him here, not you.

– Him? Him! He's where he deserves to be.

Such feelings meant mess, chaos.

'You trained me.'

That training would support him now.

– We could adopt one.

– I don't want somebody else's cast-off.

It was the same performance every morning. He watched, fascinated, as the man who was still his father and not the fool worked the blade up and down the strop. He saw again those little flicks of the wrist, those flourishes that sent the lather into the bowl or basin.

The dabbing that followed interested him most.

– A drop here and a drop there.

Under the arms; into the black bush on the chest. Sometimes the sweet-smelling water burned Daddy's cheek:

– Stronzo!

– They don't all go to pieces?

– No. The fanatics don't as a rule. They're the ones I'd have put down like dogs.

– If I die ordinary, no one will remember me.

'Go on, smile,' he said to her, looking up at the cloudless sky. He stood, smart as ever, outside the house he'd bought with hard-earned money. 'You can see underneath.'

She was long dead, thank God.

He walked briskly to the car.

Perhaps that had been his moment of glory: seeing piss run down Albert Hawker's leg.

If he thought about it, that was his biggest regret: that before Pamela there had been only tarts.

Ridiculous, with his good looks.

Crowds lined the streets. Their backs as stiff as any soldier's, Buller's slim twin daughters followed the coffin.

– You heard the one about the nun who goes to confess, Frank?

– No.

– Well, she tells the priest how the abbot from the monastery next door took her by surprise in the kitchen. 'Oh, Father,' she says, 'the two of us has

57

committed a mortal sin.' Well, the priest's eyes light up, as you can imagine, and his breathing comes on thick like and he sticks his ear up close to the grille and he asks her 'My child, was it against your will?' 'Oh no, Father, it was against the kitchen dresser and it would have done your old heart a power of good to hear them cups rattling!'

— Why doesn't he come with us?

— Who are you calling 'he'?

— Daddy.

— That's better. Because he has business to attend to. Because he's earning money so that we can eat.

— He never comes with us.

Into the cold and dark to hear the stones.

He stopped whistling.

He had rubbed one of Pamela's scents into his chest. The stuff was on his face and under his arms.

It had a sharp smell, which was a relief. These days most men put muck on themselves after shaving.

She was fat enough now. She would be gross when she started to swell.

— I took such delight in that little bird.

A tower had risen where their warmth had been.

— Mangi, mangi.

She gave him bowl after bowl of spaghetti. She jogged his arm whenever he stopped eating.

— What's she saying, Daddy?

— She says you're like a skeleton.

They came from Naples. They made their home in the poorest part of London.

Belsey stood before him for three hours.

'I need a drink.'

Belsey rolled a glass in his hands, sniffed its contents, put it to his lips and drank. Gold flashed briefly.

Of course there had been happy times. She'd laughed fit to burst over Mrs Emerald's arthritis.

— Why are you limping? Have you hurt your leg?

— It's transference.

— I'm sorry, I don't understand ...

— Have you heard my cough lately?

— No, Mrs Emerald, I don't think I have.

— I know you haven't. My friend Mrs Mason has got it.

— What has she got?

— Oh, we are slow today. Mrs Mason has got my chest cough. And I've got her arthritis. I've had it since last Wednesday. Mr Spencer's intermediary arranged it.

— If a baby dies soon after it's born, where does it go?

She gave him the look which meant he was being stupid.

— It goes to limbo.

Imagine.

Naturally he could smell her: he was reeking of her damned scent.

Wives left their husbands, husbands their wives, every single day. He was no one special. There was comfort in the thought.

It was nonsense, the very idea of his being brought low. After the things he'd seen; after all the shit he'd waded through. Frank White had vowed on just such a bright day that he would never lose control again; picture him doing so now, and for a mere woman.

'Chin up, old lad.'

Something to hope for: that familiar howl; the smug expression leaving that face for ever.

— She made fun of my warts.

— You'd have human beings put down like dogs?
    — Only those, and they're not human.
    — What are they then?
    — Mad. Evil.
    — You believe in evil?

– I've looked it in the eye. I've sat in the same room with it.

– And you've seen nothing to pity?

– You're half in love with that bloody word. You lot are all the same. You speak about things you should thank your lucky stars you haven't had dealings with –

– I only asked a question.

– No. I see nothing to pity. The world would be well rid of a few monsters.

The ghost picked up his pen and wrote.

Think of the life that had vanished from this part of London: the poky shops, the small factories, the endless lines of washing.

The criminals of the future would be coming down from the skies.

– Let me take my book with me.

He hadn't shouted when he said:

– Whatever our motives, scribbler, just imagine how safe you'd be without us. I can't see you wiping up the mess.

Her teacher now, her master. Yo ho ho.

He bought a bottle of aspirins.

He handed the tube to the receptionist.

– Oh yes, your sperm. Doctor will be in touch with you.

Perhaps it would have the ghost's ugly freckles, his crooked teeth. Perhaps, like him, it would lose its hair at an early age.

Imagine their bald daughter.

The pictures went up and their last home was declared open. The walls looked the same as all the others; the wardrobe in the corner, on top of which the fool had put their suitcases, was like all the other wardrobes in all the other rooms.

He was in the sea as soon as David looked at Nora, his body leaping and diving. The boy they could do without had vanished from himself, was gone.

– Frank, stir yourself. Fill the kettle for me.

Leafy would still be strutting up and down tomorrow. And tomorrow and tomorrow.

'Hullo ... Are you there?'

He waited.

'Mr Belsey! Charlie?'

The old man might have died.

'I've brought you some stout.'

Sparrows were making the hedges sway.

'You know where to go.'

He went into the house.

'Who's the scotsman's cocoa for?'

'Me.'

'I can't figure out why you brought me that beer.'

'May I use your toilet?'

'You'll stain the carpet if you don't.'

He took a deep breath of the honeysuckle.

There were two books on a shelf: The Pilgrim's Progress and the Complete Works of Shakespeare.

'Why don't we have our drink in the garden?'

'If that's what you want.'

'Yes, it is. I'll take the chairs out. Get some glasses.'

'Orders, orders.'

The old man told him he was amazed at his ignorance. That was begonia, that fuchsia, the tall ones were hollyhocks —

'I envy you.'

'I'd well nigh forgotten the taste of this.'

'You should be proud of yourself.'

Although he was content to be silent he said, 'You're a reading man.'

'I was.'

'I saw those books in the toilet.'

'If you're going to call here again, you'd best learn to say lavatory. Yes, I've had them as far back as I can remember.'

'I could never get on with Shakespeare.'

'I could. I did. Wisest man who ever drew breath. We used to go to his plays as a change from the music hall, the two of us, sometimes of a Saturday night, perched high up in the gods. I won't say all his words are as clear as daylight to me but I got the gist. You looked down at that stage and there were all those people, each one with a life of his own. That to me was always the marvel of it. You're wearing His Lordship's face, you are. You don't have to be cut-glass to like Shakespeare, you know.'

'I prefer to read a good war book. Something true.'

'You do, do you?'

'We had a teacher at school. We called him Leafy because his name was Leaves. He fancied himself as an actor. He used to strut up and down spouting Macbeth.'

'Was that all he taught you?'

'No. Macbeth's the only thing that comes back to me.'

And those deserts, and those islands. Those slant-eyed fiends and those brave Englishmen.

And the jeering pack that surrounded him.

'I said I had a story to tell about the other one.'

'Eh?'

'The Pilgrim's Progress.'

'Have you?'

'If you can be bothered to listen.'

'I think I can.'

The old man chuckled. 'It always used to tickle me, the thought that it once belonged to him. My father – if that's the right word. A proper piss-arse he was, according to Ma.'

'You didn't know him?'

'Ma got shot of him soon after she dropped me. He was born bone idle, she said, and a day's honest work nearly killed him. Every penny she couldn't get out of him ended up in some landlord's pockets. He took in gin, she maintained, like the rest of us takes in fresh air. Anyhow, one Sunday afternoon when I was not so much as a twinkle, he tottered into the dump they had for a home and got down on his knees and with tears the size of a dwarf's balls rolling down his cheeks he told Ma that he was a new man. He'd seen the folly of his ways, he said. The truth had dawned on him at last. "And I've heard little ducks fart before," she gave him back when he was done showering her feet. "I mean it this time," he said, and he shoved The Pilgrim's Progress into her hands. "This will put me on the path. This will put me on the path." She reminded him that he couldn't read: he was heading up a blind alley. Then he told her he'd got the divine power and went to sleep on the floor. She found out what had happened when he was a bit more capable. His money had run out in the boozer and he'd wandered into the Tabernacle up the Elephant. Spurgeon was preaching. You heard of him?'

'No.'

'You really are bloody ignorant. He was a legend, that man. As I was saying, Charlie Spurgeon was preaching. Not only was he doing that, he was giving away The Pilgrim's Progress by the cartload as well. "So that's how you came by it," Ma said. "I might have bloody known. If they was giving away camel's snot you'd be first in the queue for it."'

He filled their glasses.

'Ma was a wonder. Dead at fifty, she was, and I'm not surprised. Left me over two hundred pounds she did. That's how I bought this place.'

He heard how she made her way up from Dorset Street, in those days known as the Do-as-you-please.

'Jack the Ripper.'

'That's right. Ma was just a girl when he was at it. She knew — not to speak to, mind you — one or two of them shagbags he done for.'

He'd seen, when he was one of the chosen, a

photograph of that last victim: bits and pieces of her
– liver here, breasts there – all over the room.

'They used to say you could hear their screams for
years afterwards.'

'I'm sure they did. There are more than enough
fools in the world.'

'What are you going to do with him?'

'Who?'

'His Lordship.'

'Your son. He'll go to prison. The doctor's certain
he didn't have a brainstorm. He's sane as houses.'

'You can't be sane and do what he did.'

'Yes, you can. What a comfort it would be if every
murderer was mad.'

'I don't want to see him.'

'Tell me some more of your family's ancient
history.'

– Alec says, for all your toughness, you're really a
child.

– And what do you think?

– I think he's right.

'I had a nice juicy steak for my dinner.'

Belsey chewed.

'And what did you have?'

Belsey put a thumb to his mouth.

'Come on, let's hear from you.'

Belsey shook his head.

Tonight's sleuth was a skinny individual, more a
shadow than a man, who walked with a stoop, rolled

his own cigarettes, and wore a dirty raincoat in all weathers.

But see this apology once he's in action – there he goes, tackling a whole gang of them, each thug as brawny as a boxer. Four against one – a kick in the groin, a sharp left to the chin, a chair on the head and a twist of the hand that holds the revolver. Bang! Breathe again – the bullet's gone into the floor.

'You're too late,' says this Samson in disguise as half the police force of England rush into the warehouse. And with that he steps over a body and goes off into the night.

'Had a good day?' asks his wife as he hangs his dirty raincoat in the hall. He shrugs. 'I've done your favourite – sausage and mash.'

He choked on his whisky.

Here it is. I've typed it beautifully, you must admit.

I think it's an accurate reflection – the opinions are all yours. The style seems to me to be right too. It catches your tone of voice.

He closed the drawer.

– Come and join us!

'Damn you.'

The cart hadn't made its journey.

'Alleluia.'

He went to the window. It would soon be morning.

Clouds!

— I've heard it all so often. I could say it all for them: it was his broken home, it was his childhood, it was too much of this and not enough of that. I'm sick to my gut of their claptrap.

'Sick to death of it.'

— The way they talk, it's a wonder the whole human race isn't raping and maiming and killing. Let me ask you a question for a change — were you happy as a boy?

The ghost thought for a moment.

— Moderately.

— You were lucky. I was miserable.

He had spoken quietly. That misery was a fact. He'd gone on:

— I'm as sure as I am of anything in this world that my mother had no love for me. She didn't have any left after the Holy Trinity and my dear Daddy had taken their share. And you should have seen those rooms we lived in. Faded wallpaper, cracked lino: they stank of the failures who'd been in them. I'm weary of excuses.

— You can't expect everyone to be like you.

— Why not?

He got up from the floor. His body was beginning to ache.

– Pam was our afterthought, you might say.

– I think you'd better sit down.
  – I'm happy standing.
  – Very well.
  – Say your piece. What's His Lordship been up to?
  – Murder. His wife and son.
  The old man stared at him.
  – Thank you for bringing me the news.

No scent today. Imagine him doing that again.
  He would sell the house and make a new start.

'Feed him.'
  'Yes, sir.'

It was like a doss-house. A boy, clasping a guitar, was
asleep on the first landing.
  Lucy Belsey was naked.
  'Put some clothes on.'
  'No.'
  'You heard what I said.'
  'Yes.'
  'Cover yourself.'
  'No.'
  'Go on. Dress.'
  'I don't want to.'
  'I want you to.'
  'So?'

'You're half in love with that bloody word.'

'Perhaps.'

Her body was beautiful. Imagine —

'You disapprove? It disgusts you, my nakedness?'

He threw her a yellow towel.

'I suppose that means you wash occasionally.'

'You poor thing.' She stood up. 'Yes, you are a poor thing.' She walked towards him. 'A typical product.' She picked up what looked like a blanket with sleeves. 'Weren't you taught to avert your gaze while a lady dresses?'

'Cut the cackle.'

She dressed slowly.

'Happy now? Or is the pig disappointed?'

'This pig would be flying before he felt that. Now you're respectable again, you're coming with me to pay a visit.'

'Am I?'

'To your father.'

— He doesn't take me for granted, Frank.

Let her rack her brains.

He stopped whistling.

'Why do you hate us so much?'

'Work it out for yourself.'

'You tell me.'

'I hate the things you defend.'

'What things?'

'Property. Possessions.'

'And people's lives — '

71

'You're murderers, too. Thanks to you and your kind most of the world is starving. It's murder when a man has nothing to eat – a far worse murder, I think, than anything he did to them. Their pain lasted a few minutes. It didn't go on degrading them for years.'

'What's your cure, miss? Revolution?'

'What else?'

'People die in revolutions.'

'Aren't they dying now?'

'You're very simple.'

'I treat that as a compliment. The simplest ideas have proved to be the ones most beneficial to mankind.'

'You shouldn't call us pigs. We're only human.'

'That's just the trouble. You're not.'

He knew he was of use.

'I don't envy you your easy life. You're a child underneath that hardness. An educated baby.'

'Cars make me feel sick.'

'We're nearly there.'

Hypocrites, the lot of them: Rest in Peace; In Loving Memory; Have Mercy on the Soul of Nora White.

Cards. Scraps of paper.

Better to be a before man than an after.

Up against a barrier you came: smack!

Would he have told Buller about these memories plaguing him?

Buller would have advised him to behave like a man.
'Yes.'
But the tight bastard would not have lost control.

'A right bloody wilderness it was before I took it in hand. There was willow-herb everywhere. And bindweed, and thistles. Coltsfoot grew up that bank. Even the house was sprouting ragged robin. When I first clapped eyes on it I promised her I'd have it looking like a paradise one day.'
'Her?'
'My wife. Who did you think I meant – the Queen of Sheba?'
'What was her name?'
'Mrs Belsey.'
'That's a surprise.'
'Since you're so anxious to know, it was Pearl.'
'Unusual.'
'His Lordship thought it was common. Fit for a barmaid, he said.'
Imagine the Pearls who would read about him as they rested their feet after the Sunday rush.
'I recall how she stood here with me, all that time ago. "Paradise!" she said. "Could you picture Adam and Eve living by the side of a railway track?"'
He filled their glasses.
'I'll be nowhere, like she is, soon enough.'
'Nowhere?'
'That's the place. We come from it and we go back to it.'
'Old King Cole's a merry old soul today, I don't think.'

'I wanted her to go first. But not the way she did.'

'It was an accident. All the witnesses agreed.'

'She always maintained I'd be buried at sea, seeing as how I'd put half the ocean into me in my time.'

'It's gone home, what I said – hasn't it?'

'One afternoon, I recall, a train came to a halt up there. Signal trouble. The weather was hotter than it's been these past weeks. People were leaning out of the windows to get a better view. You could see they were taken aback. I swelled with pride then. I was pleased with myself.'

'I took her to see him.'

'Who?'

'So you aren't deaf. I took your granddaughter to see your son.'

'Did you?'

'She looked at him and he looked at her.'

'What was said?'

'He's finished with words.'

'I don't believe you.'

'Come and speak to him.'

'No. I won't and I can't. No.'

'You feel nothing?'

'What does A.H. stand for?'

'I'm not with you – '

'On your tie. Albert Hall, is it?'

'You're as slippery as the fish you eat.'

'You haven't answered me.'

'The disease is catching. Let me put you out of your misery. They're the initials of Albert Hawker.'

'I'm no wiser.'

'He murdered five little girls.'

'You caught him, did you?'

'Yes.'

'Wasn't arresting him enough, then?'

'He was special.'

'He must have been.'

Mothers, recognizing Inspector White from the newspaper photos, had shaken him by the hand in every part of London.

'I said I had a garden in my mind's eye when I was a mole.'

— And what is his book going to be about?

    — He won't say. Frank, please lose your temper.

    — Me, I suppose. I'll be his subject.

    — I don't know.

    — I do.

Thinking of those two would put him off his steak.

— Tell me frankly, Doctor, I'm a man who likes to hear the truth. Am I the sterile one?

    — You don't appear to be. But then, neither does Mrs White. You must keep trying — that's all I can recommend.

If at first you don't succeed, you never bloody will.

Suddenly, for no reason, Peter Lawson and Ronnie Taylor and John Allen ceased to be his friends. They were in the jeering pack now, surrounding him:

    — Frank's a dago!

Only Benny was constant.

Once, he remembered, Benny the Yid and Frank

the Wop – they'd heard 'wop' in a gangster film at the Super Palace – went through the City and past the docks and into those streets where the Ripper had done his dirty work.

– There's sod all to see, Frank. And the cat's piss is getting up my conk.

– You shouldn't have such a big one. Just imagine him standing here, hacking her guts out –

– Your mind!

It was Benny who explained what Lily did for a living. They plucked up courage and went to see her one December afternoon.

– I only give the full service when the weather's mild.

He told himself to sleep.

He went downstairs hours before daybreak.

*I am the man who sniffed out Albert Hawker.
Readers of the (insert name of newspaper) will remember who he is.*

*Those very same readers have probably forgotten
me already. I'm only the copper who caught him.
Does that sound bitter? Well, it's meant to. That's the
kind of world we live in, a world with its values upside
down. It's a world – and I won't mince my words –
where the man who does wrong is treated almost like a
hero, and the ordinary, decent, everyday chap has to
fight to make himself heard. The sooner we stop
glorifying thugs and villains the better – that's my
view.*

*But I don't wish to sound conceited. I'm only doing
a job. I expect no praise for it. Even so, I'm no
ordinary policeman. I deal with the murderers – the
ones who go a stage further than any other type of
criminal. I'm often asked what I would do with these
people, if I had any say in the matter. Well, I have 3
suggestions and I don't expect them to be popular.
Number One: Put down the cold-blooded fanatics as
you would put down a mad dog. I mean by fanatics
those who kill for the sheer hell of it. Number Two:
Hang or gas or shoot (I'm personally for the latter)
the thugs who rob and kill at the same time and those
brutes who mow down their protectors – and I don't
have to tell you who they are. Number Three (which
is where I differ from the hard-liners): I suggest*

78

imprisonment for at least 20 years for the men and women who lose control and murder when their tempers are at boiling point.

— Alec says Piper proved himself to be a human being.

— He would have throttled Hill, given the opportunity. Stop telling me what Alec says, what Alec thinks. Don't you have any views of your own?

— You haven't asked me for my views on a single matter — even the weather, Frank — in all the years of our marriage. Why do you want them now?

But the (insert name of newspaper) has invited me to tell my story, not just to air my opinions — and there's more opinions than common sense being aired these days, if you ask me. You never know — what I have to say about my life in the force might inspire (if that's not too airy-fairy a word) somebody's son to follow in my footsteps. I can't promise him a life of excitement and glamour, but I can say this: if you do the job well, you'll be serving your country as bravely as any soldier on the battlefield.

— Go in peace.

'Simple-minded bitch.'

— Have a malt for once.

'This is good enough for me.'

— I'll wager ten to one you won't find a better ghost.

— I'm not a betting man.

— Here's my card.

A hypocrite's scrap of paper.

In this very room, under this same lamp:

— You've confirmed all my worst prejudices.

You've about as much sympathy for common humanity as a marble slab.

 – I don't go around screwing other men's wives.

 – That I can understand. I can't imagine you being showered with invitations.

 – You won't make me lose my temper. Keep your voice down. This is a decent neighbourhood.

 – Well put. Just the pronouncement one would expect from an upholder of bourgeois morality.

 – Piss off out of my house, you parasite.

Another question people often ask me is this – isn't scientific progress in matters of detection making your kind of copper redundant? Well, yes it is, in a way – that's the answer I give them. Science makes a difficult job a bit easier. It helps us to save a lot of time and energy. But that's all. The man who dedicates his life to

Imagine their bald daughter!

who dedicates his life to tracking down vicious criminals will never be replaced by a machine.

 – It's the thrill of the chase you enjoy.

 – Is that another of Alec's thoughts?

 – No, Frank. I've been your wife for twenty years, don't forget –

 – I shall try to –

 – And I've noticed how you look while you're on the hunt. And when they're caught! It's as if you loved them –

 – You should be writing the book, not him. I don't like swearing in front of a woman, but you're talking balls.

 – That's a step forward, I suppose.

 – What is?

80

– You've found the courage to say a rude word to your little woman.

No thrills. No love. But a matter of urgency, yes: get them in case they strike again.

Last week I treated readers of the (insert name of newspaper) to a bit of a sermon. Well, even coppers have to let off steam at times.

'The bastard.'

I'm not saying I'm a hero

'And I never did.'

I don't want to sound dramatic, but I've looked evil in the eye

'I have, I have.'

I'm a before man, not an after.

– Would you be happy if there were no murderers?

– That's a ridiculous question.

– No, no. Just imagine a world in which people never lose control – to quote your phrase. Every man loves his neighbour, lives and lets live, and universal harmony is the order of the day. Would you be happy with such a world?

– I'd be round the twist if I said no. Yes.

– What job would you do?

– Oh, I'd find something ...

– Butcher, baker, candlestick maker?

– Let's get back to the business in hand, shall we?

Next week I shall tell readers of the (insert name of newspaper) how I caught Albert Hawker.

Under this same lamp:

– I've heard enough of your pity bullshit. Years ago I got into the one and only blind rage of my life. My fool of a father was bragging that we would soon be rolling in it: when this deal was clinched we

would be living in style. Style! I've told you about
those rooms. I looked at my mother. She was –
After all, a dog with rabies is put down and
– She was pretending to believe him.

There she stood, supporting him – which she never
failed to do. Could she have a new costume when the
money came? Or a new day dress, perhaps, to replace
her old polka? Yes, yes. Why not? Why not?
I would go so far as to call it mercy-killing.

– You've done well for yourself.
– Yes.
– Nice wife.
– Yes.
– Not a job I'd have chosen –

Be kind to the poor sod, he told himself. Don't
mock the afflicted. Don't say what he's half expect-
ing.

– I shan't get mixed up with crooked men no
more. I mean it. I mean it.

Then, with his voice down in his boots:

– I don't like to ask you, Frank, but –
– You're in need of what you call a "loan"?
– No, no, no. A reference, Frank – that's all I
want from you. A few words on a piece of paper. Just
tell them they can trust me. I promise you I won't
let you down.

– Don't then.
– It will look very good for me, a reference from
a policeman –

One small wound:

– You've grown fat. You're the image of your
babbo.

People change.

He asked the ghost what the joke was.

– Hill and Hawker. It sounds like an act on the halls.

– There was nothing funny about them.

– Or an old-established firm. "I always buy my shirts at Hill and Hawker's."

Only wrecks drank whisky in the middle of the night.

'Scotsman's cocoa.'

Think of Belsey's father. Imagine the state of his mind after his Pearl had been run over.

Albert Hawker had no idea of the difference between right and wrong. He told the court he was playing games.

Witnesses said she was dragged several yards along the ground, her shopping bag still in her hand.

Speaking as one who saw how those games ended, I

A woman said the driver seemed to change colour, even though he was as black as the ace of spades.

– Oh yes, His Lordship sent flowers. His wreath well nigh covered the grave. And he crossed the river, too – along with Her Ladyship and the heir apparent – and came here and said how sorry he was, the hypocrite.

'Is this me?'

When he left the house in the morning he would be the tight bastard again. At the moment, though, he was an unrecognizable mess, all feeling and no sense.

People often ask me for my

'No, they don't.'

– Alec says you're as vengeful as a child.

This week I'm going to give you some straight-from-

the-shoulder opinions on the subject of do-gooders. To hear some of these people talk, you would think that being a murderer was a respectable way of life. Well, I've heard what they've got to say. I know their arguments backwards by now. They can just shut up and listen to me for a change.

The trouble with the velvet paws brigade is this – they don't have to go in and clean the mess up like I had to. They would soon change their tune if they saw the state of some of the victims of their heroes. The mothers of the little girls who crossed Albert Hawker's path know what I mean. Try telling them about his broken home and his unhappy childhood, you clergymen and psychiatrists. You'll get the answer you deserve, that's for sure.

– You look at me with the same pair of eyes.
(Sorry and all that. I've only just remembered these are supposed to be the considered thoughts of your retirement. Ask the editor of the (insert name of newspaper) to put Episode 1 into the past tense: 'I was no ordinary policeman', etc., etc. On we go –)

She stood there, pretending to believe him – as was her custom.

His training ground: those rooms where the failures had been. His trainer: a mother who never pretended to him; who never told him comforting lies.

– Did you confess all your sins?
Mr Pickard poured him a glass of lemonade.
– Yes.
– Are you sure?
– Yes, Mummy.
Cards arrived at Adastra House.

– Come and see Mr Spencer one evening when you're off duty. I'm certain he could make contact for you.

Well, I'm sick to my gut of their excuses.

He awoke.

In another part of London a man was hiding in a cupboard under some stairs while a hyena paced up and down a hallway, taunting him, braying.

'WHAT A storm that was. There's air to breathe
again now. You look like you were out in it.'

'No, I don't.'

'I wasn't referring to your clothes. You're still the
same tailor's dummy you were yesterday. I mean the
expression on your chops.'

'What's the matter with it?'

'I'd swear you'd seen a ghost.'

The laugh got past his teeth.

'Yes. I have.'

'A funny one, was he?'

'Bloody hilarious.'

'You must tell me where he hangs out. When
you've stopped laughing, that is.'

'Fetch the glasses.'

'Orders, orders.'

He placed the chairs on the lawn.

'Why do you keep coming here? If it's to find out
why His Lordship did what he did, you might just as
well ask the man in the moon.'

'He wrote "No More Words" on a piece of paper.'

'That was clever of him.'

'Your son.'

'I was wondering who you meant: what you said
was giving me a lovely picture. I never dreamed
there'd come a day when His Lordship would be
happy with his trap shut.'

'People change.'

'So they say. Some don't, though. I thought His Lordship was one of them.'

'His name is James. Or Jim, perhaps. Or even Jimmy.'

'Not to me, it isn't. I wouldn't worry about him if I was you. He'll be spewing, rest assured, when the mood hits him.'

He surprised himself by saying, 'No, he won't. He's done with words for ever.'

'Mind-reader, are you?'

'It's a feeling I have.'

'You put your trust in a thing like that?'

'I'm only human.'

'He broke my Pearl's heart.'

'How?'

'How? How? It would take me all sodding night to tell you how.'

'I'll have a cup of tea for breakfast.'

'What's it to you?'

'I might learn something.'

'Pigs might fly.'

'Yes. Imagine.'

'Oh, the past's best forgotten.'

'You remembered a lot of it yesterday.'

The old man had been a mole again, in the Flanders trenches, cursing the thrushes twittering in the sky that was like a sheet of steel.

He recalled, too, hearing a nightingale once, singing high up in what was left of a tree. Its song was as good as a bath while it lasted.

'Come on, Charlie.'

And then that greenness. There was a lull. Fighting stopped. The generals were having a

88

chinwag somewhere and the Boche had sent a
message to God to turn off the water-works. The sun
shone on the moles as they came up out of the mud.
They walked for a bit and saw grass. There were
bushes; there were trees – they could scarcely credit
it – with leaves on. For a few blessed days it was as if
they were in England. He kicked a ball about with
Tom Gadny and Sam Wormbey and Harry Roberts
and other mates. The officers played cricket.

'Force yourself.'

They had water, what was more. They stood in
those wash-houses and scrubbed and scrubbed. They
were whiter than the whitewash on the wall by the
time they were done.

'You're as bad as him for not listening. You ask
me to tell you how and then you go off into space.'

'I'm sorry, Charlie.'

'You're very familiar all of a sudden.'

'I beg your pardon. Where had you got to?'

'Your trance is over, is it?'

'Yes'.

'I was saying about him looking down on us. He'd
hardly begun at his second school before he was
putting us in our places and making it clear to Pearl
and me how ignorant we were. He jumped at every
chance to show off what he'd learnt.'

'You should have been proud of him.'

'Who's supposed to be talking – me or you?'

'Carry on.'

'We were proud of him all right, as you're so anxious
to know. Christ, it wasn't his book learning that griped
us. We wanted a brainy son. Is your arm asleep?'

'No.'

'Top my glass up, then.'

'I was hanging on your every word.'

'Careful. There's more froth than beer.'

'My hand seems to have the shakes.'

'So I see. Thanks. No, it was his attitude, not his brains. He was going to make his way in the world; "be a somebody" was his expression. He wouldn't be content with the life of a mousy clerk, saying yes, sir, yes, sir, three bags full. He'd have people saying that to him. It was that remark finished him for me. I called him His Lordship then, and have done ever since.'

'Were you a mousy clerk?'

'I was a clerk, yes. And a good one too. I worked for a firm of solicitors – Jarman and Company. In all the thirty-odd years I was with them I never called Old Jarman "sir". I was polite, as was proper, but that's different. I don't hold with arse-crawling. I kept my distance. If His Lordship had bothered to listen – no, even if he had listened, he wouldn't have understood.'

He wouldn't have understood that his father, over there, had seen just how equal all men are. A duke's guts look much like a dustman's.

One of the bits of fodder that hadn't been eaten, he returned to England himself all over. His Ma had been working on the trams, due to the shortage of men. He trudged up and down the streets of London and after weeks of climbing stairs and knocking on doors he got fixed up with Jarman and Company. He would earn enough for his mother to have a rest. Perhaps he would find a nice girl to marry ...

90

His Lordship wouldn't have understood that the day he and his Pearl found this house and the wilderness behind it, he had wanted nothing else from life but the peace and quiet of living here, and making flowers grow where weeds had been, and sharing her love.

He watched the old man grill the kippers.

'That was the last time we saw him.'

'What was?'

'Didn't I say?'

'No.'

'I must be going gaga. Oh, it was a few years back. We got invited, the two of us, to their state apartments. Out of the blue it came, his letter. I was for tearing it up and not involving ourselves, but Pearl's nature was of the forgiving kind: something might be gained from pouring oil on the troubled waters, she said. So we went. Her Ladyship was done up finer than the dog's dinner – all she lacked, Pearl remarked after, was a tirara. It was lovely to see us again, how well we were looking, what a beautiful dress Pearl was wearing – it made me heave to hear her. And the heir apparent was bobbing up and down, pouring beer and offering us filthy-looking things on sticks – a right little St Vitus. Worst of the lot was him. I asked myself, I recall, what his behaviour was in aid of – why should he be acting the long lost son to his common old father?'

'Did you find out?'

'Bloody sure I did. I was there, and so was my Pearl, for the benefit of the guests. We was the show. My God, they were a la-di-da pair – '

91

'The guests?'

'I wish you'd stop interrupting me. Yes – the guests, like I said. His name was Quentin, but I forget what hers was: it had a handle in front of it, that I do remember. Dad and Mum were the free entertainment, it soon became obvious. I nearly jumped out of my skin when His Lordship asked me to tell Quentin and Horsemoosh my Pilgrim's Progress story.

'Here you are. It's a bit burnt round the edges, but the rest of it's good and nourishing.'

'Thank you. Did you tell the story?'

'Yes, to my shame. And others. But not with any relish. His Lordship sat guzzling his brandy and boasting as how he was a Cockney, born within the sound of Bow bells, the hypocrite. And Horsemoosh told me a thousand times I was the salt of the earth.'

The old man began to eat noisily.

'She did fish for us that night – '

'Her Ladyship? I mean, your son's wife – '

'You were right first time. She cooked us a sole, I recall. Not that you'd have known, by the taste of it. It was like eating glue. Looked like it as well.'

'I enjoyed that.'

He savoured the whisky instead of swallowing it.

'We had trouble getting my fish during the last war. That frozen stuff stank of ammonia. Whale I never took to. A mammal, isn't it?'

'Yes. At least, I think so.'

'I learned that from His Lordship. Corrected me, he did, when he was no higher than the chair you're sitting in. In that voice of his.'

'Which I've yet to hear.'

'I'd count myself lucky if I was you.'

The old man carried the plates to the sink.

'I've fathered a murderer. It's only just struck me.'

'My mother was beautiful. She was thin and fair; the looks of an angel. She was of Irish descent. County Cork. She never set foot there. Her father – '

– I want him here, not you.

'Her father, she told me, made his name in London, in the wine business. He was a teetotaller.'

'That sounds proper Irish, that does.'

He wiped her spit from his face.

– Where is he? Where is he?

– You know where he is.

Tears were starting. He was going to be less than a man.

'You in your trance again?'

'No.'

'Ask the cat to give you your tongue back.'

'Oh, you don't want to hear my ancient history.'

'It's better than staring at the wall.'

'Her father gave her away in church – '

'Your mother?'

'Yes. Not the Queen of Sheba.'

'What's unusual about that?'

'Nothing. It's what happened afterwards, when they got outside. He said to her "You've got him now" – meaning my father – "Let him keep you." Then he bundled his wife and his two other daughters into a car and off he went.'

'Married beneath her, had she?'

'Yes. Dear Daddy's family weren't well-off at all. Italians. They came here from Naples.'

'Foreigners who settle usually make a good living.'

'They had a little shop. They sold candles and sweets; not much else.'

Warmth there: the spaghetti with tomatoes bubbling on a black stove.

'Gone now. A tower block's been put up in its place.'

He found himself laughing.

'My parents were such snobs.'

'Like His Lordship?'

'Very like. Worse, probably. Dear Daddy was so ashamed of his origins he changed his name. David White.'

'Wanted to pass for English, did he?'

'Yes, indeed he did. An English gentleman.'

– "Oh, oh, Antonio, he's gone away ... "

'I asked him once for an explanation. Esposito – that's the real one – was as common as Smith, he said: two a penny in Italy. I looked the word up in a dictionary at the library. There was a bit more to it. 'Foundling' was what it meant. You know, a child who is – '

'I know all right. I'm not as bleeding ignorant as I look.'

'Daddy wanted finer ancestors.'

'And how was your mother stuck up?'

'She couldn't forget her childhood; the luxury. She wanted a mansion but she got rooms instead. One after another, in practically every part of London. Wherever we stayed she always gave the other boarders the cold shoulder.'   ·

94

'Dead, him and her, are they?'

'She is. He's not.'

'Lives with you, does he?'

'No. He's in a Home.'

'I see. You've swept him under the carpet.'

'You don't see. I've put him out of harm's way. It's a nice place – near the coast. Beautiful gardens. Every convenience.'

'Silent as the grave, sir.'

HE TOOK off his Albert Hawker tie and blew into his shirt. He lay back and followed the adventures of the tightest bastard imaginable, tighter by far than yours truly. But wait. What's this? Insults, threats, the voice rising to a scream almost; even a sharp slap across the villain's kisser: this man, at the height of his career, has no discipline, no patience, no control. He heard himself saying to the screen, 'Keep your distance. Calm down.'

Pamela's junk was all over the house. Creams and scents in the bathroom, glass animals in the lounge. And that stupid mare Melissa was still by his bed, not with the flies.

'Damn you.'

The joke of it was he had stopped desiring her years ago, five at least by his count. Those nips of gin while she grilled his steaks, those chocolates — they had done their work. Sometimes, making love to her, he had had to force a picture of her young body into his mind.

That picture came easily to him now.

Let her claw. Let her moan.

'She's fat. She's ugly.'

But she glowed before him.

He had his pride.

And so, the story went round the district, had Mrs Pickard. She stood like a ramrod in the court. Her husband Sidney was a good man. He was a firm believer in education. She would wait for his return because she loved him.

The Threepenny Tosser went to prison for a long stretch.

'Poor sod.'

Listen to him. Imagine if he and Pamela had had a son and that son had met up with a Mr Pickard ...

Six prisoners had set on that bent individual and given him the beating of his life.

He was no one special. There was comfort in the thought. The woman he would have left her for was somewhere in the world.

'Alec says!'

Alec wrote:

Hill and Hawker weren't the only ones I brought to justice. Readers of the (insert name of newspaper) will probably remember Edmunds the strangler, or Long the poisoner.

'Up them stairs, old lad.'

He shut the drawer.

Then, one wet morning, he let those moments go from him.

– Get up, Frank. We'll be late for Mass.

She had the missal in her hand.

He got out of bed slowly. He took an apple from his coat pocket, rubbed it on his pyjama sleeve, and bit into it.

– You know you mustn't eat before –

– I'm not coming with you.

– Yes, you are, Frank. Stir yourself.

His father snored.

– Take him.

– Stop being silly now. There's sleep in your eyes still. Be quiet at the basin so you don't disturb him. Come along.

– No.

She was too startled to speak. He had a mind of his own, he said. Angels up above and devils and waiting in limbo was a lot of nonsense; tripe, if she wanted his opinion.

He had to break the silence.

A baby born to a woman who hadn't been got at by a man – in his opinion, that was daft too.

He put into words – feebly; they had no power to express his feelings – the sea and sky, the leaps and dives, the red of the sun. God had been with him at Margate, but nowhere else and never again afterwards.

She smiled.

He was empty once they were gone from him.

He remembered his sudden loneliness. He felt the positive chill of it.

She did not mention hell or sin. One thing was certain, she said – if you were born a Catholic you stayed one for ever. You could blaspheme, you could try to break away, but you stayed one neverthe-less.

He ate the apple core.
No prayers.
'No.'
And no blessings. And flames would lick his lean, strong body when the time came.

RIGHT HAND to left foot; left hand to right – the day wouldn't dawn when he'd be the image of his father.

He drank black coffee. He took a shower. He dressed carefully. He brushed his hair. Everything was in order.

London was behind him. He stopped whistling.

Trees. Fields. Birds.

'Peace.'

What about retiring to the country?

'We'll see, old lad.'

Learning the names of flowers? Making them grow?

'I haven't the patience.'

'Would you like a cup of tea?'

He'd prefer scotsman's cocoa.

'If it's no trouble.'

'Do sit down. I shan't be long.'

There must have been warmth here once. He lifted the lid of the piano stool – it was crammed tight with music.

'I do apologize for not being able to see you earlier. The shock, you know.'

'I understand.'

'Do take a scone. Cook made them before she went on holiday.'

'Thank you.'

'The tea's not too weak?'

'It's delicious.'

'Harrods blend it for me. I can't say that the shock has passed but I am confident I shan't blub. I do so hate people displaying emotions.'

'Yes.'

'I do hope your journey here was pleasant.'

'It was very nice. I enjoyed the scenery.'

'You must take a stroll along the front. In normal circumstances I would be sitting in my deck-chair near the Grand with my old fogy friends. You know?'

'Yes.'

'We're spared the riff-raff, thank God. Marian's daughter paid me a visit in April. She brought a so-called man with her.'

Yo ho ho.

'I gave them hospitality. They didn't bother to disguise the fact that they were laughing at me — they made no effort at all. I do persist in believing that manners count for something.'

'Yes.'

'They do help us to keep so many dreadful things at bay. I must climb down from the pulpit and offer you another cup.'

'Thank you, Mrs Paget.'

'Life can be a messy business at times. However, one doesn't expect ... No sugar?'

'No.'

'Do eat up the scones. My appetite's gone on strike.'

'Just one more.'

'I can't say I was enamoured of James. I did respect him, though. He was an industrious man. He saw to it that Marian lived in comfort.'

The slaughterhouse.

'Marian loved him very much. I was never in any doubt about that.'

Imagine.

Yes, she replied, she played that instrument. It was in need of repair, like herself. It was her custom to batter poor Chopin on it every evening after dinner.

Impossible to build sandcastles down there.

He walked a mile or more without seeing a single child.

He whistled as he drove into the oven.

'I want to give you some money for that beer.'
'Forget it.'
'I don't approve of charity.'
'A token of friendship.'
'Is that what it is?'
'Yes.'
'Am I the best you could find?'
'Drink.'

'No, Charlie, my father didn't fight for his adopted

country. He had what he called "a dicky ticker".'

'They're always popular when a war's brewing.'

'Whenever people told him to go back to Eytie-land he used to say, "I am English like roast beef." Sometimes it was, "Like roast beef I am English." He said he was English like steak and kidney pudding on one occasion. Poor fool.'

Listen to him!

'Spineless, gutless wreck.'

'That's no way to talk of your father.'

'Have you heard Charles Oswald Belsey on the subject of James Harold?'

'That's different altogether.'

'He fought for nothing and no one.'

'How did he keep his family?'

'I'd love to hear his answer to that question. He worked on and off, mostly the latter. He sold brushes from door to door for a while. Then he got involved with some astute men of business. They were Daddy's downfall. In and out of prison he went – a few nylons, or piffling sums of money. And he was ashamed of his decent parents, remember. He only visited them when he was on the scrounge. I went with him – less than half a dozen times. I was sworn to secrecy. Mother must never find out.'

'Your wife can't be seeing much of you these days.'

'How did you know I was married?'

'The eyes in my head told me. Or is the wedding ring for show?'

'She doesn't see much of me. She sees sod all. She's gone.'

'Not dead?'

'No. She might soon want to be. She left me for another man. Mr Alec Turner. A ghost by profession.'

'Haunts folk for a living, does he?'

'Well put. Strictly speaking, Charlie, he helps men like me who have a story to tell but lack the words to tell it with. I was right round the bend when I gratefully accepted his kind offer. Promises, flattery: he gave me the whole bloody works. He would sell my memoirs to a barmaids' bible as soon as I collected my pension and settled down to a life of retirement.'

Let her try mental cruelty.

'Clean your ears out. I said I feel sorry for you.'

'Spare me your pity. I'll survive.'

'As you please then.'

'I trusted him. I'd known him in a vague way for a number of years. He'd written up some of my past glories.'

'Glories, eh? I bet you have trouble finding a hat to fit you.'

'I was joking.'

'Oh, you were. Give me fair warning before you crack the next one.'

'Pour your own stout.'

'She didn't want her big little son to be a policeman.'

'The danger, was it?'

'She had no fear for my safety.' He spoke quietly: it was a fact. 'Now I think about it, it was because she was married to a man whose deceit was transparent, clear as daylight. Yes, that must have been the reason.'

– In your element.

'He was in prison when she died.'

– You know where he is.

'She told me to piss off. She crossed herself after she said it.'

In the street, on that bright day, people were running to shelter.

'The war was on.'

'He would have made a good general, His Lordship would have.'

'She got her last rites. She's with her angels.'

'No, he didn't just murder them. He played games. Do I have to put it in words?'

'You wouldn't class His Lordship with him?'

'He's taken two lives.'

'I've fathered a murderer.'

'Suicide was still a crime in those days. I had this good friend, a sergeant; his name was Buller. I went with him on his rounds one Christmas Eve. I had to be thrown in at the deep end; see a few corpses, get accustomed to the sight. "They all fall flat during the festive season" – he should have had it carved in wood, he said it so often.'

They were living things, and warm.

'The first I saw was a girl with golden hair – the image of your granddaughter. It shocked me, I remember, that someone so beautiful should have cause to die.'

Those wicked nuns frolicked at Buller's command.

'The last that night was a woman who looked like

a man. She'd made a noose out of six regimental ties. Ridiculous. The patrons of the Prince Albert knew her as the brigadier. Buller said she wouldn't be going on manoeuvres any more. He'd known her well.'

— You'll be wading through shit.

'I started off by catching a strangler. He told me she poked fun at his warts.'

'Fancy a kipper?'

'My appetite's on strike.'

'Let's be going then.'

'Going? You? Where?'

'You've won.'

No glory.

'I want to take a look at him.'

'Your son?'

'His Lordship.'

'It's time you told me why the pictures are turned to the wall.'

'Pearl. I'm with her in a couple of them. So's he. I can't stomach looking at her herself all over.'

'I understand.'

'Help me into my jacket.'

'It's loose on you.'

'No matter. Is it safe to lock up?'

'Of course.'

'Easy for you to say. They're waiting with their bulldozers.'

'You won't be away for long.'

'They could step in at any time. They're watching.'

108

'Where from? That rubble? Don't be silly, Charlie.'

The old man pressed his body against the door.

'Is it fast?'

'Yes, Charlie.'

'Sure, are you?'

'As I am of anything.'

'I'm not in the mind to trim those hedges.'

'We'll stop at a chemist. I know one not far from here.'

'Need a rubber raincoat, do you?'

'Not at all. I want to buy you a present. Some bars of soap. Water isn't enough. You smell, Charlie.'

The old man said he'd known, in his heart of hearts, it was an accident. Pearl had forgotten to look both ways.

He'd stomached death over there. He'd had to. But the thought of her lying mangled in the street, near the shops, on a day like any other – it made his insides do a turn about.

And now His Lordship. Where was the sense of it? Gone out of the window, like the man with no trousers who hadn't the money to pay the tart.

The smile would vanish.

'I'm glad I'm only on a visit.'

'I've seen worse.'

'This place looks bad enough.'

'They don't run a mission here. It isn't meant to be a home from home.'

'The interview room is it, sir?'

'No. The cell.'

The old man stared at his son.

'What happened to you?'

'Tell your father.'

'I'll listen.'

Belsey put a finger to his lips.

'Face up to it. Now come on. Spill the beans to me.'

Belsey shook his head.

'Nothing to say?'

Belsey nodded.

The old man walked across to the bed.

'There must be something. In Christ's name. There has to be something.'

The old man got down on his knees. He took his son's hands and kissed them. Then he kissed his cheek. Then his hair.

'Jim.'

Belsey pushed his father aside.

He helped the weeping old man to his feet.

'You can drive me back.'

'That was my intention anyway.'

'Safely delivered.'

'I'll pretend to myself you're the Jehovah's Witness if you drop by here again.'

'What do you mean?'

'What I mean is, you'll find the door bolted. I want you to leave me alone. Thanks for the soap. Now I'll be able to sniff myself where I haven't dared sniff for months.'

'GIVE ME your arm.'

'Arm?'

'Yes. A.R.M.'

'Why should I give it to you?'

'Do you want to stay on the ground?'

'Did I ... ?'

'Pass out? I presume so. You're not dressed like a gentleman of the road.'

'I think I can manage by myself – '

'You obviously can't.'

'Are you going to help me, or aren't you?'

'Yes. If you'll let me.'

'Here.'

'Have you been to a party?'

'Party!'

'I take it you haven't.'

'No. No party.'

'A private celebration?'

'Yes. That's what it was.'

'You've grazed your forehead. I'll clean it up for you. Where do you live?'

'I can look after myself. You go about your business. You go on your way.'

'Is it far?'

'You heard me. Push off.'

'You can't manage on your own. You'll fall down again. How far from here is your home?'

'I can cope. I bloody can.'

'Bon voyage.'

'Is this the High Street?'

'Yes.'

'Third turning to the left.'

'In which direction?'

'Oh, straight ahead.'

'Oh, yes.'

'Ridiculous.'

'Yes. You shouldn't drink so heavily.'

'Me being led along like some cripple. That's what's ridiculous. Never thought the day would dawn.'

'Steady.'

'You could do with a haircut.'

'You're in need of something too.'

'It's nearly as long as Ben Gunn's. Yo ho ho.'

'Don't shout. We'll get water thrown over us.'

'Respectable neighbourhood.'

'Very. All chintz and closed curtains.'

'Wives behind them being unfaithful.'

'Only when their hubbies are off for the firm in foreign parts.'

'Fat lot you know. You'd be surprised.'

'Are you an expert on the subject?'

'I bloody am. I bloody well am.'

'Sh.'

'Tambourine. Ridiculous.'

'That's your favourite word.'

'You're right. I'm half in love with it.'

'Which house is yours?'

'Twenty-seven.'

'Will your family be up?'

'Place is empty.'

'Do you live alone?'

'I do.'

'Whoa. Give me the key. I hope it isn't lost.'

'I'm quite capable of – '

'Try the other pocket.'

'Orders, orders. It should be in this one.'

'Do as I suggest.'

'Well, that's the first time it's ever been in there. I'll open my own front door, if you don't mind.'

'The lock's at the edge. You'll break the glass.'

'It's mine to break. There! See. I was capable.'

'I'll come in with you.'

'Invitation only. Scram.'

'Such gratitude. Where's the light?'

'Up in Annie's room behind the clock.'

'Of course. I see it. Your eyes are a lovely shade of scarlet.'

'Ever tried tying up those ringlets of yours with a piece of ribbon?'

'Yes. Lead me to the bathroom.'

'Want to powder your nose?'

'Let's get there and find out.'

'I put her muck under my arms. Rubbed it into my chest.'

'Did you?'

'I bloody did.'

'Quiet now. Think of those respectable wives behind their curtains.'

'Imagine.'

'Aren't you going to open your own bathroom door?'

'You're not useless.'

'Thanks.'

'Et lux perpetua.'

'Over we go. Get down. Hold on to the side. Shove two fingers down your throat. You'll feel better in the morning.'

'A proper Florence Nightingale, aren't you?'

'Drink this.'

'I'd rather have scotsman's cocoa.'

'Florence wouldn't advise it.'

'One nip.'

'No.'

'Orders.'

'Yes.'

'It's nearly three. What were you doing out so late?'

'I like walking in cities at night.'

'Looking for company?'

'I meet people sometimes.'

'Are you bent?'

'Be more specific.'

'Can't you understand plain language? Are you a queer?'

'You're still not precise enough.'

'Are you a pansy boy?'

'Well, I don't wriggle like that. No, my hands don't flop in that manner either.'

'Answer my question.'

'In plain language, I prefer making love to men.'

'I'm a policeman.'

'I'd come to the conclusion that you weren't an actor.'

'Would you have helped me if you'd known what

116

I did for a living?"

'Yes. Why not?'

'You call us pigs.'

'The word hasn't passed my lips. You were drunk and incapable so I did what I could for you.'

'Tell me your name.'

'Piers.'

'Sounds very cut-glass.'

'Doesn't it? But then, I am the son of a gentleman farmer. Yeoman stock.'

'Will you follow in his footsteps?'

'I plough a different furrow. Real pigs – as distinct from imaginary ones – hold no interest for me.'

'Do you think I'm handsome?'

'Yes.'

'Attractive?'

'Yes. I fancy you.'

'You'd better not try anything on with me, young man. I'd knock you into the middle of next week.'

'I shan't. Have no fear.'

'I'm not afraid. It's you who should be.'

'I shall try my hardest to look terrified.'

'I don't often get drunk.'

'That's good news.'

'I usually know when to stop.'

'I'm sure you do.'

'Lately I've been hearing voices. I seem to be losing all control of my feelings.'

'It's the change of life, I expect. Have you had any hot flushes?'

'You're making fun of me.'

'No, I'm not.'

'I keep going cold. Ridiculous, in this heat.'

'Whisky won't cure you.'

'I shall be all right. Drink's speaking. Chin up.'

'Don't touch that cut. You'll have it bleeding again.'

'Yes, Nurse. I'm tired.'

'Florence recommends sleep. Go to bed. I'll say goodbye.'

'My name's Frank.'

'Go and rest.'

'I shall only dream. I just want to lie down. Stay with me and talk.'

'Upstairs?'

'Upstairs.'

'You can get into bed. There's room enough for you to keep your distance.'

Skin smooth to the touch. No hairs, except for those in the obvious places.

A living thing, and warm.

Oh, and why not? Sailors on long voyages, hairy ballocky Barnacle Bills – they got into the habit.

Oh, a wild, wild lad.

Thugs, brawny as boxers, became shit-shearers on long stretches.

No one else could possibly know. If, by some chance, he was found out – well, there were plenty of excuses. He was pissed when it happened, drunk as a lord, he might have been on Mars. Those flowing locks, those ringlets – you'd have sworn it was a girl. These days they should carry banners saying

what they are. Even had its legs up, the way some
women like it. What's more, it had tits of a kind –
well, a bit bigger than you normally see on men. The
skin was smooth, smooth.

'I'm terrified.'

It lived and was warm and he had grown accustomed to embracing ice.

'Frank. Frank.'

He could say 'Florence.'

'Are you happy?'

'Aren't you?'

'I shall be all right.'

'Not the future, Frank. Now.'

Thank God the light was out.

'I don't feel so bad.'

'Such charm.'

'I can't kiss you.'

'I thought, as it's so dark, you'd forgotten who I
am. My name's Piers.'

'I stop at that.'

'So many do. Take your time.'

Closed curtains.

It had no stubble on its face, this creature.

'I want you to say it.'

'Say? What?'

'My name.'

With so many excuses, it was easier to kiss.

More warmth.

He was wrapped up like a mummy.

Usually, when he awoke, the bedspread was on the floor. The top sheet, too, was usually nowhere near his body.

He freed himself. He could breathe and exercise.

Dear Frank,

I am just about to tiptoe away by the dawn's early light. Or am I? Consulting my watch, I see it's already after eight. Missed it again! What a very good time-keeper the Chevalier de Rouget was.

I decided not to wake you – for my own peace of mind as much as for yours. I know a randy Puritan when I see one. Your post-coital misery would have been quite insufferable to me.

I gathered from your nocturnal mumblings that you are of Italian descent. Strange. If anyone's soul needed bathing in Mediterranean sunlight it's yours, my dear (those last two words were penned without an accompanying gesture). Yes, Frank – soul, not body.

You are very handsome. I was surprised to learn that you're a detective (same mumblings, as above – section devoted to past glories) – you don't have that heavy, paunchy look I associate with the word. A cliché, of course – like your dismaying impression of a homosexual. Your later performance had the ring of truth about it – on the surface.

Your nurse, whose name is Piers, recommends a good cry. Let your chin drop.

You mentioned Heathcliff whilst we were entangled. Don't emulate him. Such a messy life.

I wonder if you realize that you practically bit my nipples off.

120

I've made a note of your phone number. I might ring you in the future.

Thank you. Ciao. Piers.

P.S. I wish all my lovers had your taste in bedside literature. I've left the book on the kitchen table. I haven't laughed so much for a long while. That scene when the old duke whips Melissa!!!

HE ASKED the warder to leave him alone with Belsey.

'I'm a man who trusts his first impressions of people. I know for a fact you're as sane as houses. You lost control. This madness of yours, this refusal to speak — it's a sham, a pretence. You're wily. A sharp businessman like you knows his onions. "No more words" means "Unfit to plead", which means you'll be carted off to one of the bins where you'll be treated and fed. People, reading the papers, will say you went out of your mind. You'll receive their pity.

'I'll pay you a compliment. I've had a feeling, these last few days, that the world's madder than I'd previously supposed. Your beautiful daughter waiting for the revolution — I wonder if she'll fight when the barricades are up. She's mad. She looked at your two victims, her own flesh and blood, and twitched. That was all. A marble slab. And Charles Oswald — he's nuttier than a fruit cake when the mood's on him, isn't he? Compared to them, you're a model of sanity.

'Why didn't you kill them? It would have made more sense. No, you gave way to a common impulse. You let it take over for a little while, before the light returned. I've had that impulse. I stood in front of my father, like I'm standing in front of you now, and I put my hands on his throat. I started to throttle him as I'm starting to throttle you. I stopped. There —

I've stopped again. Control. You slaughtered the nearest to hand, didn't you?

'There's remorse behind that smile. There's mess in your head. Chaos. I can see the torment you're in.

'I want you to summon up a scrap of courage. Let me make an example of you. Pay the penalty. The world has to go on. Behave like a man and face the music.

'I shall respect you if you cry. The worst murderer I ever came across – he chopped two women into pieces: even he had a tear to spare for his canary.'

'No booze for you tonight, old lad.'

– Alec has opened my eyes.

– Busy man. He's opened something else of yours as well.

She glowed before him on the dance floor. They waltzed.

He shivered.

Mr Clayton, pipe in one side of his mouth, said:

– Pam was our afterthought, you might say. I was fifty, and Alice – who did most of the work – was forty-two when she came along to brighten our lives.

Sandcastles crumbled.

'Not a drop.'

There was snow on the ground. Hard yellow dog turds crackled underfoot. He looked at the Russian on the carpet and Buller told him the story of the nun with the cucumber.

He looked at Albert Hawker's book. An ostrich, a young toff in a top hat, a boy with golliwog's hair.

He looked at the bodies in the slaughterhouse.

He looked at the red forest and heard the tambourine.

He saw Sandra and Jennifer.

Piper had lost control. Piper had wept. The sights were too much for him.

Her feet were in the cellar. One leg was on the stairs, the other on the landing. Her torso was in the

126

bedroom. Her hands were on the attic mantlepiece, on either side of her head.

– I took such delight in that little bird.

Ridiculous, with all he'd seen, to be brought low by a mere woman.

'Fat bitch.'

To have this crop of regrets.

– If he had no idea of right and wrong, why did he piss himself when you arrested him?

– Fear of authority.

– I see.

'You didn't bloody see. Not for a minute you didn't.'

A hypocrite's scrap of paper, like those cards that came to Adastra House.

– Very thoughtful. Very touching.

– Her sisters sent them, Mrs Emerald. They shunned her in life.

– It's never too late to make amends.

– How do they know I live here?

– Fate.

Ridiculous Mrs Emerald, with her mulled wine each Christmas Eve:

– Bertie was such a connoisseur. I warm it in his memory, and to celebrate the season.

And her visits to Mr Spencer:

– I wish Mrs Mason would come back from Broadstairs. Her arthritis is crippling me. My chest cough's a luxury by comparison.

Perhaps Mr Spencer could call his intermediary out of nowhere and do another swap.

Let her try mental cruelty.

Cold struck his body: he didn't desire her; he

127

didn't want her company. Catch him going where
the ghost had been.

Imagine their bald daughter.

'Not even a nip.'

— Having that tie made!

— He was special.

— The way you all drank after you caught him.

— If we'd had a child ... Just think.

— The way you all crowed.

'You never bloody saw.'

'Sh.'

He dropped what was left of the steak in the dust-
bin. He buried Melissa in the muck.

— He's talking his gibberish again.

Imagine them, young, coming from Naples.

Their Davide. Her David.

'Transparent fool.'

Imagine the mole returning. Picture him on the
water.

— I couldn't stomach meat any more. That bully
beef we had to get down us finished me. That, and
the smell of horseflesh.

'Don't give in. It stays where it is. Above the
label.'

— He ought to be hanged. Made an example of,
said Mrs Paget.

If he didn't want her company, what future
awaited him?

— Where is he? Where is he?

— You know where he is.

— You didn't try to get him out. Did you? To see
me once, before I ...

— I've no power.

– I want him here, not you. Piss off.

Revenge: the stones.

'Dominus bloody vobiscum.'

He listened. The respectable neighbourhood was silent.

He had grown accustomed to the worst men were capable of.

I'm not saying I'm a hero

'I never bloody did.'

We see your nightmares in broad daylight –

'I said that.'

He had a collection of comics. He used them as bait.

There was a pool at Albert Hawker's feet.

Well, the time has come to wind up. I'm going to be an ordinary bloke from now on, living a quiet life with the missus. I hope readers of the (insert name of self-righteous rag) have enjoyed this heap of shit.

He would send her that last page.

He tore up the rest of the manuscript.

He shattered every scent bottle.

Cats, deer, mice, elephants – he destroyed them all.

'Silence reigns.'

He would sleep on the settee.

He awoke. The cart hadn't made its journey.

He listened. The voices had stopped.

He was empty.

He heard himself laugh. He wanted them back

again: the ghost arguing, Pamela screaming, the fool being English like roast beef. He wanted to feel her spit on his face. He wanted to defend himself.

Ice embraced him. Its clutch made him yearn for the darkness the cart had so often tipped him into.

HE HAD run out of clean shirts. He would have to look a bit grubby for once.

Not even the thought of Buller could warm him: that good man, his one true friend, so senselessly mown down in the course of duty.

Pamela had belittled him as well – the man whose death she had mourned with so much show. Alec had said something.

He felt no anger.

He took the knife from the kitchen drawer and wrapped it in brown paper. He put it in his case.

He was left alone with Belsey in the interview room.

'What did your mother look like? A blowsy barmaid with a shelf stuck out in front?'

Gold flashed briefly.

He sat and waited.

He stared at Belsey. The smile had vanished.

The lips were moving. The eyes had narrowed.

He saw the back of Belsey's mouth.

He heard a howl.

Belsey had made his way in the world. He'd

climbed high. Here he was, reduced now, a wreck; something less than a man.

He opened the case and put the knife, still wrapped in brown paper, on the table.

'That's the best present you've ever been given.'

He slammed the door behind him.

'He's broken down. Let him have a few minutes to himself.'

The man whom Piper had called a tight bastard lay on the grass enjoying the warmth of the sun.

He yawned and stretched and felt contented. Ducks, flying low, passed over him.

Ice was melting in the great oven.

There was no one in the house.

He would write to her while he still felt warm. He walked to the desk, treading glass into the carpet.

He began:

Dear Pamela,

By all means have your divorce. I hope you give birth to a fine baby.

Alec Turner isn't worthy of you, but that has nothing to do with me.

Thanks for the good times.

With best wishes for the future.

FRANK

He tore up the last page of the manuscript before going out to post the letter.

He was clearing up the mess in the bathroom when they came for him.

'HE'S ON the danger list,' said Nash.

'Will he pull through?'

'We'll hear tonight.'

'I wanted to give him his dignity back.'

'It's Jenkins who's in danger of his life, not Belsey.'

'Jenkins?'

'The warder. The man looking after that mad sod.'

'Oh God, no. Oh good God, no. No, no.'

'Yes. Jenkins was on the receiving end of your knife.'

'No.'

'Yes, I say.'

He would try to put it in words. He would find the necessary courage. He would help the police with their inquiries.